THE CHRISTMAS CARD CRIME

and Other Stories

edited and introduced by
MARTIN EDWARDS

BRITISH LIBRARY

First published in 2018 by
The British Library
96 Euston Road
London NW1 2DB

Cataloguing in Publication Data
A catalogue record for this publication is available from the British Library

ISBN 978 0 7123 5247 5
eISBN 978 0 7123 6463 8

Typeset by Tetragon, London
Printed and bound by CPI Group (UK) Ltd, Croydon CR0 4YY

THE CHRISTMAS CARD CRIME

and Other Stories

CONTENTS

INTRODUCTION

Welcome to the third anthology of winter mysteries to be published in the British Library's series of Crime Classics. This collection brings together eleven stories written over the span of more than half a century, and features a mix of leading exponents of detective fiction and some less renowned names. The stories, some of which have never been republished subsequent to their original appearance in print, are equally diverse.

The publication of this book brings up to a round dozen the number of short story collections that have appeared in the Crime Classics series. Sales have far exceeded the levels traditionally associated with anthologies, whether in the crime genre or otherwise, and this is surely a cause for delight. It has long been the received wisdom within the publishing industry that "short stories don't sell", but this has always struck me as a self-fulfilling prophecy that deserves to be challenged.

It's thought-provoking to reflect that as long ago as 1956, the introduction to the very first anthology of short fiction published under the aegis of the Crime Writers' Association pronounced, with regret, that the outlook for the short story was "bleak". Forty years after that, I took over as editor of the CWA anthology, and I'm pleased to report that it's still going strong. So the doom-mongers should, surely, think again.

I'm one of many readers (and writers) who love short stories, and in an era of allegedly brief attention spans, it seems extraordinary that the vast commercial potential of short fiction has yet to be fully realized. I hope that other publishers will follow the

British Library's admirable lead in the field of publishing (and marketing enthusiastically) anthologies of crime fiction, just as they have proved keen to supply the ever-growing demand for vintage detective story reprints sparked by the worldwide success of so many titles in the Crime Classics series.

The difference between a short story and a novel is not merely a question of length. The two forms are different in *kind*; you might compare it to the difference between having the whole Sistine Chapel to paint and a commission to produce a small miniature. From a writer's perspective, there simply isn't the time or space to indulge in leisurely description or painstaking elaboration of character and motive. With a novel, if a few words are wasted, no-one is likely to worry. With a short story, or at least with the better short stories, every word must be made to earn its keep.

Writers often say that writing a short story is harder work than writing a novel. If it's an exaggeration, it nevertheless has a kernel of truth. And there are plenty of financial reasons to prefer writing novels to short stories. Indeed, these considerations led the late H.R.F. Keating, a distinguished and prolific author of both novels and short stories, to say in his book on *Writing Crime Fiction*, that the advice he was tempted to give when asked about writing short stories was—"don't." But he readily acknowledged that short stories have a special appeal, and they offer a good many benefits to writers. For instance, one can experiment with a style, setting, or set of characters that might not suit a novel, or justify the investment of time that it takes to write a full-length book. Moreover, writing short stories can help to refine one's literary craft.

The crime genre seems to me to be particularly well suited to the short form. Indeed, detective fiction as we understand it really began with short stories, written by the American master Edgar

Allan Poe. And although Wilkie Collins wrote outstanding novels, it's fair to say that until the First World War, the dominant form of detective fiction was the short story. Later, things changed, but crime writers continued to enjoy trying their hand at short stories.

Some wrote a great many—among the contributors to this volume, examples include Baroness Orczy, John Dickson Carr, Cyril Hare, and Julian Symons. In contrast, the short stories of E.C.R. Lorac, John Bude, and John Bingham were few and far between. And whilst connoisseurs of the genre may have come across some of the contributions previously, I suspect that few will have encountered those by Bude or Bingham, let alone the title story, 'The Christmas Card Crime', by a writer who faded from view many years ago; his work strikes me as enjoyable and undeserving of such neglect.

This collection, therefore, amounts to a seasonal assortment box offering a great deal to whet the appetite during the cold winter months. In researching the ingredients, I have been assisted by fellow enthusiasts John Cooper, Jamie Sturgeon, Nigel Moss, as well as Gerald Verner's son Chris and his agent Philip Harbottle. I'd like to thank them, and Rob Davies and his diligent team in the publications department at the British Library, for their support. Books about John Dickson Carr, and Francis Durbridge, by Douglas G. Greene and Melvyn Barnes have also provided me with valuable background information. I've much enjoyed compiling this particular assortment box, and hope that readers will derive equal pleasure from devouring its contents, whether at Christmas or any other time of the year.

MARTIN EDWARDS
www.martinedwardsbooks.com

A CHRISTMAS TRAGEDY

Baroness Orczy

Today, Baroness Orczy (1865–1947) is remembered, if at all, as the creator of Sir Percy Blakeney, alias "the Scarlet Pimpernel", dashing hero of a long series of wildly popular historical romances set at the time of the French Revolution. Ultimately, she became so successful that she was able to move to live in luxury in Monte Carlo. But she first achieved distinction as an author of short crime stories in the early years of the twentieth century, having arrived in Britain from her native Hungary in 1880. Her reputation reached such heights that she was invited to become a founder member of the prestigious Detection Club, formed in 1930. Although by that time her day as a detective writer was past, and she made an annual pilgrimage from her home by the Mediterranean to dine with fellow Club members, the likes of Agatha Christie, Dorothy L. Sayers, Ronald Knox, and John Dickson Carr.

Orczy created a number of detectives. The Old Man in the Corner is the most renowned; in all, he appeared in three collections of stories. The exploits of Patrick Mulligan, an Irish lawyer, were ultimately collected in a book with the improbable title *Skin o' My Tooth*. *Lady Molly of Scotland Yard* (1910) recorded the eponymous heroine's battle to achieve justice for her disgraced husband. Her rapid rise to the top of the Metropolitan Police at a time when true gender equality was scarcely imaginable represents one of the most remarkable career ascents in the whole crime genre. This story first appeared in *Cassell's Magazine* in December 1909.

IT WAS A FAIRLY MERRY CHRISTMAS PARTY, ALTHOUGH THE surliness of our host somewhat marred the festivities. But imagine two such beautiful young women as my own dear lady and Margaret Ceely, and a Christmas Eve Cinderella in the beautiful ball-room at Clevere Hall, and you will understand that even Major Ceely's well-known cantankerous temper could not altogether spoil the merriment of a good, old-fashioned festive gathering.

It is a far cry from a Christmas Eve party to a series of cattle-maiming outrages, yet I am forced to mention these now, for although they were ultimately proved to have no connection with the murder of the unfortunate Major, yet they were undoubtedly the means whereby the miscreant was enabled to accomplish the horrible deed with surety, swiftness, and—as it turned out afterwards—a very grave chance of immunity.

Everyone in the neighbourhood had been taking the keenest possible interest in those dastardly outrages against innocent animals. They were either the work of desperate ruffians who stick at nothing in order to obtain a few shillings, or else of madmen with weird propensities for purposeless crimes.

Once or twice suspicious characters had been seen lurking about in the fields, and on more than one occasion a cart was heard in the middle of the night driving away at furious speed. Whenever this occurred the discovery of a fresh outrage was sure to follow, but, so far, the miscreants had succeeded in baffling not only the police, but also the many farm hands who had formed themselves into a band of volunteer watchmen, determined to bring the cattle maimers to justice.

We had all been talking about these mysterious events during the dinner which preceded the dance at Clevere Hall; but later on, when the young people had assembled, and when the first strains of "The Merry Widow" waltz had set us aglow with prospective enjoyment, the unpleasant topic was wholly forgotten.

The guests went away early, Major Ceely, as usual, doing nothing to detain them; and by midnight all of us who were staying in the house had gone up to bed.

My dear lady and I shared a bedroom and dressing-room together, our windows giving on the front. Clevere Hall is, as you know, not very far from York, on the other side of Bishopthorpe, and is one of the finest old mansions in the neighbourhood, its only disadvantage being that, in spite of the gardens being very extensive in the rear, the front of the house lies very near the road.

It was about two hours after I had switched off the electric light and called out "Good-night" to my dear lady, that something roused me out of my first sleep. Suddenly I felt very wide-awake, and sat up in bed. Most unmistakably—though still from some considerable distance along the road—came the sound of a cart being driven at unusual speed.

Evidently my dear lady was also awake. She jumped out of bed and, drawing aside the curtains, looked out of the window. The same idea had, of course, flashed upon us both at the very moment of waking: all the conversation anent the cattle-maimers and their cart, which we had heard since our arrival at Clevere, recurring to our minds simultaneously.

I had joined Lady Molly beside the window, and I don't know how many minutes we remained there in observation, not more than two probably, for anon the sound of the cart died away in the distance along a side road. Suddenly we were startled with a terrible cry of "Murder! Help! Help!" issuing from the other side of the house, followed by an awful, deadly silence. I stood there near the window shivering with terror, while my dear lady, having already turned on the light, was hastily slipping into some clothes.

The cry had, of course, aroused the entire household, but my dear lady was even then the first to get downstairs, and to reach the garden door at the back of the house, whence the weird and despairing cry had undoubtedly proceeded.

That door was wide open. Two steps lead from it to the terraced walk which borders the house on that side, and along these steps Major Ceely was lying, face downwards, with arms outstretched, and a terrible wound between his shoulder-blades.

A gun was lying close by—his own. It was easy to conjecture that he, too, hearing the rumble of the wheels, had run out, gun in hand, meaning, no doubt, to effect, or at least to help, in the capture of the escaping criminals. Someone had been lying in wait for him; that was obvious—someone who had perhaps waited and watched for this special opportunity for days, or even weeks, in order to catch the unfortunate man unawares.

Well, it were useless to recapitulate all the various little incidents which occurred from the moment when Lady Molly and the butler first lifted the Major's lifeless body from the terrace steps until that instant when Miss Ceely, with remarkable coolness and presence of mind, gave what details she could of the terrible event to the local police inspector and to the doctor, both hastily summoned.

These little incidents, with but slight variations, occur in every instance when a crime has been committed. The broad facts alone are of weird and paramount interest.

Major Ceely was dead. He had been stabbed with amazing sureness and terrible violence in the back. The weapon used must have been some sort of heavy clasp knife. The murdered man was now lying in his own bedroom upstairs, even as the Christmas bells on that cold, crisp morning sent cheering echoes through the stillness of the air.

We had, of course, left the house, as had all the other guests. Everyone felt the deepest possible sympathy for the beautiful young girl who had been so full of the joy of living but a few hours ago, and was now the pivot round which revolved the weird shadow of tragedy, of curious suspicions and of an ever-growing mystery. But at such times all strangers, acquaintances, and even friends in a house, are only an additional burden to an already overwhelming load of sorrow and of trouble.

We took up our quarters at the "Black Swan," in York. The local superintendent, hearing that Lady Molly had been actually a guest at Clevere on the night of the murder, had asked her to remain in the neighbourhood.

There was no doubt that she could easily obtain the chief's consent to assist the local police in the elucidation of this extraordinary crime. At this time both her reputation and her remarkable powers were at their zenith, and there was not a single member of the entire police force in the kingdom who would not have availed himself gladly of her help when confronted with a seemingly impenetrable mystery.

That the murder of Major Ceely threatened to become such no one could deny. In cases of this sort, when no robbery of any kind has accompanied the graver crime, it is the duty of the police and also of the coroner to try to find out, first and foremost, what possible motive there could be behind so cowardly an assault; and among motives, of course, deadly hatred, revenge, and animosity stand paramount.

But here the police were at once confronted with the terrible difficulty, not of discovering whether Major Ceely had an enemy at all, but rather which, of all those people who owed him a grudge, hated him sufficiently to risk hanging for the sake of getting him out of the way.

As a matter of fact, the unfortunate Major was one of those miserable people who seem to live in a state of perpetual enmity with everything and everybody. Morning, noon and night he grumbled, and when he did not grumble he quarrelled either with his own daughter or with the people of his household, or with his neighbours.

I had often heard about him and his eccentric, disagreeable ways from Lady Molly, who had known him for many years. She—like everybody in the county who otherwise would have shunned the old man—kept up a semblance of friendship with him for the sake of the daughter.

Margaret Ceely was a singularly beautiful girl, and as the Major was reputed to be very wealthy, these two facts perhaps combined to prevent the irascible gentleman from living in quite so complete an isolation as he would have wished.

Mammas of marriageable young men vied with one another in their welcome to Miss Ceely at garden parties, dances and bazaars. Indeed, Margaret had been surrounded with admirers ever since she had come out of the schoolroom. Needless to say, the cantankerous Major received these pretenders to his daughter's hand not only with insolent disdain, but at times even with violent opposition.

In spite of this the moths fluttered round the candle, and amongst this venturesome tribe none stood out more prominently than Mr Laurence Smethick, son of the M.P. for the Pakethorpe division. Some folk there were who vowed that the young people were secretly engaged, in spite of the fact that Margaret was an outrageous flirt and openly encouraged more than one of her crowd of adorers.

Be that as it may, one thing was very certain—namely, that Major Ceely did not approve of Mr Smethick any more than he did of the others, and there had been more than one quarrel between the young man and his prospective father-in-law.

On that memorable Christmas Eve at Clevere none of us could fail to notice his absence; whilst Margaret, on the other hand, had shown marked predilection for the society of Captain Glynne, who, since the sudden death of his cousin, Viscount Heslington, Lord Ullesthorpe's only son (who was killed in the hunting field last October, if you remember), had become heir to the earldom and its £40,000 a year.

Personally, I strongly disapproved of Margaret's behaviour the night of the dance; her attitude with regard to Mr Smethick—whose constant attendance on her had justified the rumour that they were engaged—being more than callous.

On that morning of December 24th—Christmas Eve, in fact— the young man had called at Clevere. I remember seeing him just as he was being shown into the boudoir downstairs. A few moments later the sound of angry voices rose with appalling distinctness from that room. We all tried not to listen, yet could not fail to hear Major Ceely's overbearing words of rudeness to the visitor, who, it seems, had merely asked to see Miss Ceely, and had been most unexpect- edly confronted by the irascible and extremely disagreeable Major. Of course, the young man speedily lost his temper, too, and the whole incident ended with a very unpleasant quarrel between the two men in the hall, and with the Major peremptorily forbidding Mr Smethick ever to darken his doors again.

On that night Major Ceely was murdered.

II

Of course, at first, no one attached any importance to this weird coincidence. The very thought of connecting the idea of murder with that of the personality of a bright, good-looking young Yorkshireman like Mr Smethick seemed, indeed, preposterous, and with one accord all of us who were practically witnesses to the quarrel between the two men, tacitly agreed to say nothing at all about it at the inquest, unless we were absolutely obliged to do so on oath.

In view of the Major's terrible temper, this quarrel, mind you, had not the importance which it otherwise would have had; and we all flattered ourselves that we had well succeeded in parrying the coroner's questions.

The verdict at the inquest was against some person or persons unknown; and I, for one, was very glad that young Smethick's name had not been mentioned in connection with this terrible crime.

Two days later the superintendent at Bishopthorpe sent an urgent telephone message to Lady Molly, begging her to come to the police-station immediately. We had the use of a motor all the while that we stayed at the "Black Swan," and in less than ten minutes we were bowling along at express speed towards Bishopthorpe.

On arrival we were immediately shown into Superintendent Etty's private room behind the office. He was there talking with Danvers—who had recently come down from London. In a corner of the room, sitting very straight on a high-backed chair, was a youngish woman of the servant class, who, as we entered, cast a quick, and I thought suspicious, glance at us both.

She was dressed in a coat and skirt of shabby-looking black, and although her face might have been called good-looking—for she had fine, dark eyes—her entire appearance was distinctly repellent. It suggested slatternliness in an unusual degree: there were holes in her shoes and in her stockings, the sleeve of her coat was half unsewn, and the braid on her skirt hung in loops all round the bottom. She had very red and very coarse-looking hands, and undoubtedly there was a furtive expression in her eyes, which, when she began speaking, changed to one of defiance.

Etty came forward with great alacrity when my dear lady entered. He looked perturbed, and seemed greatly relieved at sight of her.

"She is the wife of one of the outdoor men at Clevere," he explained rapidly to Lady Molly, nodding in the direction of the young woman, "and she has come here with such a queer tale that I thought you would like to hear it."

"She knows something about the murder?" asked Lady Molly.

"Noa! I didn't say that!" here interposed the woman roughly, "doan't you go and tell no lies, Master Inspector. I thought as how you might wish to know what my husband saw on the night when the Major was murdered, that's all; and I've come to tell you."

"Why didn't your husband come himself?" asked Lady Molly.

"Oh, Haggett ain't well enough—he—" she began explaining with a careless shrug of her shoulders, "so to speak—"

"The fact of the matter is, my lady," interposed Etty, "this woman's husband is half-witted. I believe he is only kept on in the garden because he is very strong and can help with the digging. It is because his testimony is so little to be relied on that I wished to consult you as to how we should act in the matter.

"Tell this lady what you have just told us, Mrs Haggett, will you?" said Etty curtly.

Again that quick, suspicious glance shot into the woman's eyes. Lady Molly took the chair which Danvers had brought forward for her, and sat down opposite Mrs Haggett, fixing her earnest, calm gaze upon her.

"There's not much to tell," said the woman sullenly. "Haggett is certainly queer in his head sometimes, and when he is queer he goes wandering about the place of nights."

"Yes?" said my lady, for Mrs Haggett had paused awhile and now seemed unwilling to proceed.

"Well!" she resumed with sudden determination, "he had got one of his queer fits on on Christmas Eve, and didn't come in till long after midnight. He told me as how he'd seen a young gentleman prowling about the garden on the terrace side. He heard the cry of 'Murder!' and 'Help!' soon after that, and ran in home because he was frightened."

"Home?" asked Lady Molly, quietly, "where is home?"

"The cottage where we live. Just back of the kitchen garden."

"Why didn't you tell all this to the superintendent before?"

"Because Haggett only told me last night, when he seemed less queer-like. He is mighty silent when the fits are on him."

"Did he know who the gentleman was whom he saw?"

"No, ma'am—I don't suppose he did—leastways, he wouldn't say—but—"

"Yes? But?"

"He found this in the garden yesterday," said the woman, holding out a screw of paper which apparently she had held tightly clutched up to now, "and maybe that's what brought Christmas Eve and the murder back to his mind."

Lady Molly took the thing from her and undid the soiled bit of paper with her dainty fingers. The next moment she held up for Etty's inspection a beautiful ring composed of an exquisitely carved moonstone surrounded with diamonds of unusual brilliance.

At the moment the setting and the stones themselves were marred by scraps of sticky mud which clung to them, the ring obviously having lain on the ground and perhaps been trampled on for some days, and then been only very partially washed.

"At any rate, you can find out the ownership of the ring," commented my dear lady after awhile, in answer to Etty's silent attitude of expectancy. "There would be no harm in that."

Then she turned once more to the woman.

"I'll walk with you to your cottage, if I may," she said decisively, "and have a chat with your husband. Is he at home?"

I thought Mrs Haggett took this suggestion with marked reluctance. I could well imagine, from her own personal appearance, that her home was most unlikely to be in a fit state for a lady's visit. However, she could, of course, do nothing but obey, and, after a few muttered words of grudging acquiescence, she rose from her chair and stalked towards the door, leaving my lady to follow as she chose.

Before going, however, she turned and shot an angry glance at Etty.

"You'll give me back the ring, Master Inspector," she said with her usual tone of sullen defiance. "'Findings is keepings,' you know."

"I am afraid not," replied Etty curtly; "but there's always the reward offered by Miss Ceely for information which would lead to the apprehension of her father's murderer. You may get that, you know. It is a hundred pounds."

"Yes! I know that," she remarked dryly, as, without further comment, she finally went out of the room.

III

My dear lady came back very disappointed from her interview with Haggett.

It seems that he was indeed half-witted—almost an imbecile, in fact, with but a few lucid intervals, of which this present day was one. But, of course, his testimony was practically valueless.

He reiterated the story already told by his wife, adding no details. He had seen a young gentleman roaming on the terraced walk on the night of the murder. He did not know who the young gentleman was. He was going homeward when he heard the cry of "Murder!" and ran to his cottage because he was frightened. He picked up the ring yesterday in the perennial border below the terrace and gave it to his wife.

Two of these brief statements made by the imbecile were easily proved to be true, and my dear lady had ascertained this before she returned to me. One of the Clevere under-gardeners said he had seen Haggett running home in the small hours of that fateful Christmas morning. He himself had been on the watch for the cattle-maimers that night, and remembered the little circumstance quite plainly. He added that Haggett certainly looked to be in a panic.

Then Newby, another outdoor man at the Hall, saw Haggett pick up the ring in the perennial border, and advised him to take it to the police.

Somehow, all of us who were so interested in that terrible Christmas tragedy felt strangely perturbed at all this. No names had been mentioned as yet, but whenever my dear lady and I looked at one another, or whenever we talked to Etty or Danvers, we all felt that a certain name, one particular personality, was lurking at the back of all our minds.

The two men, of course, had no sentimental scruples to worry them. Taking the Haggett story merely as a clue, they worked diligently on that, with the result that twenty-four hours later Etty appeared in our private room at the "Black Swan" and calmly informed us that he had just got a warrant out against Mr Laurence Smethick on a charge of murder, and was on his way even now to effect the arrest.

"Mr Smethick did *not* murder Major Ceely," was Lady Molly's firm and only comment when she heard the news.

"Well, my lady, that's as it may be!" rejoined Etty, speaking with that deference with which the entire force invariably addressed my dear lady; "but we have collected a sufficiency of evidence, at any rate, to justify the arrest, and, in my opinion, enough of it to hang any man. Mr Smethick purchased the moonstone and diamond ring at Nicholson's in Coney Street about a week ago. He was seen abroad on Christmas Eve by several persons, loitering round the gates at Clevere Hall, somewhere about the time when the guests were leaving after the dance, and again some few moments after the first cry of 'Murder!' had been heard. His own valet admits that his master did not get home that night until long after 2 a.m., whilst even Miss Granard here won't deny that there was a terrible quarrel between Mr Smethick and Major Ceely less than twenty-four hours before the latter was murdered."

Lady Molly offered no remark to this array of facts which Etty thus pitilessly marshalled before us, but I could not refrain from exclaiming:

"Mr Smethick is innocent, I am sure."

"I hope, for his sake, he may be," retorted Etty gravely, "but somehow 'tis a pity that he don't seem able to give a good account of himself between midnight and two o'clock that Christmas morning."

"Oh!" I ejaculated, "what does he say about that?"

"Nothing," replied the man dryly; "that's just the trouble."

Well, of course, as you who read the papers will doubtless remember, Mr Laurence Smethick, son of Colonel Smethick, M.P., of Pakethorpe Hall, Yorks, was arrested on the charge of having murdered Major Ceely on the night of December 24-25, and, after the usual magisterial inquiry, was duly committed to stand his trial at the next York assizes.

I remember well that throughout his preliminary ordeal young Smethick bore himself like one who had given up all hope of refuting the terrible charges brought against him, and, I must say, the formidable number of witnesses which the police brought up against him more than explained that attitude.

Of course, Haggett was not called, but, as it happened, there were plenty of people to swear that Mr Laurence Smethick was seen loitering round the gates of Clevere Hall after the guests had departed on Christmas Eve. The head gardener, who lives at the lodge, actually spoke to him, and Captain Glynne, leaning out of his brougham window, was heard to exclaim:

"Hallo, Smethick, what are you doing here at this time of night?"

And there were others, too.

To Captain Glynne's credit, be it here recorded, he tried his best to deny having recognized his unfortunate friend in the dark. Pressed by the magistrate, he said obstinately:

"I thought at the time that it was Mr Smethick standing by the lodge gates, but on thinking the matter over I feel sure that I was mistaken."

On the other hand, what stood dead against young Smethick was, firstly, the question of the ring, and then the fact that he was seen in the immediate neighbourhood of Clevere, both at midnight and again at about two, when some men who had been on the watch for cattle-maimers saw him walking away rapidly in the direction of Pakethorpe.

What was, of course, unexplainable and very terrible to witness was Mr Smethick's obstinate silence with regard to his own movements during those fatal hours on that night. He did not contradict those who said that they had seen him at about midnight near the gates of Clevere, nor his own valet's statements as to the hour when he returned home. All he said was that he could not account for what he did between the time when the guests left the Hall and he himself went back to Pakethorpe. He realized the danger in which he stood, and what caused him to be silent about a matter which might mean life or death to him could not easily be conjectured.

The ownership of the ring he could not and did not dispute. He had lost it in the grounds of Clevere, he said. But the jeweller in Coney Street swore that he had sold the ring to Mr Smethick on December 18, whilst it was a well-known and an admitted fact that the young man had not openly been inside the gates of Clevere for over a fortnight before that.

On this evidence Laurence Smethick was committed for trial. Though the actual weapon with which the unfortunate Major had been stabbed had not been found nor its ownership traced, there was such a vast array of circumstantial evidence against the young man that bail was refused.

He had, on the advice of his solicitor, Mr Grayson—one of the ablest lawyers in York—reserved his defence, and on that miserable afternoon at the close of the year we all filed out of the crowded court, feeling terribly depressed and anxious.

IV

My dear lady and I walked back to our hotel in silence. Our hearts seemed to weigh heavily within us. We felt mortally sorry for that good-looking young Yorkshireman, who, we were convinced, was innocent, yet at the same time seemed involved in a tangled web of deadly circumstances from which he seemed quite unable to extricate himself.

We did not feel like discussing the matter in the open streets, neither did we make any comment when presently, in a block in the traffic in Coney Street, we saw Margaret Ceely driving her smart dog-cart; whilst sitting beside her, and talking with great earnestness close to her ear, sat Captain Glynne.

She was in deep mourning, and had obviously been doing some shopping, for she was surrounded with parcels; so perhaps it was hypercritical to blame her. Yet somehow it struck me that just at the moment when there hung in the balance the life and honour of a man with whose name her own had oft been linked by popular rumour, it showed more than callous contempt for his welfare to be seen driving about with another man who, since his sudden access to fortune, had undoubtedly become a rival in her favours.

When we arrived at the "Black Swan" we were surprised to hear that Mr Grayson had called to see my dear lady, and was upstairs waiting.

Lady Molly ran up to our sitting-room and greeted him with marked cordiality. Mr Grayson is an elderly, dry-looking man, but he looked visibly affected, and it was some time before he seemed able to plunge into the subject which had brought him hither. He fidgeted in his chair, and started talking about the weather.

"I am not here in a strictly professional capacity, you know," said Lady Molly presently, with a kindly smile and with a view to helping him out of his embarrassment. "Our police, I fear me, have an exaggerated view of my capabilities, and the men here asked me unofficially to remain in the neighbourhood and to give them my advice if they should require it. Our chief is very lenient to me and has allowed me to stay. Therefore if there is anything I can do—"

"Indeed, indeed there is!" ejaculated Mr Grayson with sudden energy. "From all I hear, there is not another soul in the kingdom but you who can save this innocent man from the gallows."

My dear lady heaved a little sigh of satisfaction. She had all along wanted to have a more important finger in that Yorkshire pie.

"Mr Smethick?" she said.

"Yes; my unfortunate young client," replied the lawyer. "I may as well tell you," he resumed after a slight pause, during which he seemed to pull himself together, "as briefly as possible what occurred on December 24 last and on the following Christmas morning. You will then understand the terrible plight in which my client finds himself, and how impossible it is for him to explain his actions on that eventful night. You will understand, also, why I have come to ask your help and your advice. Mr Smethick considered himself engaged to Miss Ceely. The engagement had not been made public because of Major Ceely's anticipated opposition, but the young people had been very intimate, and many letters had passed between them. On the morning of the 24th Mr Smethick called at the Hall, his intention then being merely to present his *fiancée* with the ring you know of. You remember the unfortunate *contretemps* that occurred—I mean the unprovoked quarrel sought by Major Ceely with my poor client, ending with the irascible old man forbidding Mr Smethick the house.

"My client walked out of Clevere feeling, as you may well imagine, very wrathful; on the doorstep, just as he was leaving, he met Miss Margaret, and told her very briefly what had occurred. She took the matter very lightly at first, but finally became more serious, and ended the brief interview with the request that, since he could not come to the dance after what had occurred, he should come and see her afterwards, meeting her in the gardens soon after midnight. She would not take the ring from him then, but talked a good deal of sentiment about Christmas morning, asking him to bring the ring to her at night, and also the letters which she had written to him. Well—you can guess the rest."

Lady Molly nodded thoughtfully.

"Miss Ceely was playing a double game," continued Mr Grayson, earnestly. "She was determined to break off all relationship with Mr Smethick, for she had transferred her volatile affections to Captain Glynne, who had lately become heir to an earldom and £40,000 a year. Under the guise of sentimental twaddle she got my unfortunate client to meet her at night in the grounds of Clevere and to give up to her the letters which might have compromised her in the eyes of her new lover. At two o'clock a.m. Major Ceely was murdered by one of his numerous enemies; as to which I do not know, nor does Mr Smethick. He had just parted from Miss Ceely at the very moment when the first cry of 'Murder!' roused Clevere from its slumbers. This she could confirm if she only would, for the two were still in sight of each other, she inside the gates, he just a little way down the road. Mr Smethick saw Margaret Ceely run rapidly back towards the house. He waited about a little while, half hesitating what to do; then he reflected that his presence might be embarrassing, or even compromising to her whom, in spite of all, he still loved dearly; and knowing that there were plenty of men in and about the house to render what assistance was necessary, he finally turned his steps and went home a broken-hearted man, since she had given him the go-by, taken her letters away, and flung contemptuously into the mud the ring he had bought for her."

The lawyer paused, mopping his forehead and gazing with whole-souled earnestness at my lady's beautiful, thoughtful face.

"Has Mr Smethick spoken to Miss Ceely since?" asked Lady Molly, after awhile.

"No, but I did," replied the lawyer.

"What was her attitude?"

"One of bitter and callous contempt. She denies my unfortunate client's story from beginning to end—declares that she never saw him after she bade him 'good-morning' on the doorstep of Clevere Hall when she heard of his unfortunate quarrel with her father. Nay, more, she scornfully calls the whole tale a cowardly attempt to shield a dastardly crime behind a still more dastardly libel on a defenceless girl."

We were all silent now, buried in thought which none of us

would have cared to translate into words. That the *impasse* seemed indeed hopeless no one could deny.

The tower of damning evidence against the unfortunate young man had indeed been built by remorseless circumstances with no faltering hand.

Margaret Ceely alone could have saved him, but with brutal indifference she preferred the sacrifice of an innocent man's life and honour to that of her own chances of a brilliant marriage. There are such women in the world; thank God I have never met any but that one!

Yet am I wrong when I say that she alone could save the unfortunate young man, who throughout was behaving with such consummate gallantry, refusing to give his own explanation of the events that occurred on that Christmas morning unless she chooses first to tell the tale. There was one present now in the dingy little room at the "Black Swan" who could disentangle that weird skein of coincidences, if any human being not gifted with miraculous powers could indeed do it at this eleventh hour.

She now said gently:

"What would you like me to do in this matter, Mr Grayson? And why have you come to me rather than to the police?"

"How can I go with this tale to the police?" he ejaculated in obvious despair. "Would they not also look upon it as a dastardly libel on a woman's reputation? We have no proofs, remember, and Miss Ceely denies the whole story from first to last. No, no!" he exclaimed with wonderful fervour. "I came to you because I have heard of your marvellous gifts, your extraordinary intuition. Someone murdered Major Ceely! It was not my old friend Colonel Smethick's son. Find out who it was, then! I beg of you, find out who it was!"

He fell back in his chair, broken down with grief. With inexpressible gentleness Lady Molly went up to him and placed her beautiful white hands on his shoulder.

"I will do my best, Mr Grayson."

V

We remained alone and singularly quiet the whole of that evening. That my dear lady's active brain was hard at work I could guess by the brilliance of her eyes, and that sort of absolute stillness in her person through which one could almost feel the delicate nerves vibrating.

The story told her by the lawyer had moved her singularly. Mind you, she had always been morally convinced of young Smethick's innocence, but in her the professional woman always fought hard battles against the sentimentalist, and in this instance the overwhelming circumstantial evidence and the conviction of her superiors had forced her to accept the young man's guilt as something out of her ken.

By his silence, too, the young man had tacitly confessed; and if a man is perceived on the very scene of a crime, both before it has been committed and directly afterwards; if something admittedly belonging to him is found within three yards of where the murderer must have stood; if, added to this, he has had a bitter quarrel with the victim, and can give no account of his actions or whereabouts during the fatal time, it were vain to cling to optimistic beliefs in that same man's innocence.

But now matters had assumed an altogether different aspect. The story told by Mr Smethick's lawyer had all the appearance of truth. Margaret Ceely's character, her callousness on the very day when her late *fiancé* stood in the dock, her quick transference of her affections to the richer man, all made the account of the events on Christmas night as told by Mr Grayson extremely plausible.

No wonder my dear lady was buried in thought.

"I shall have to take the threads up from the beginning, Mary," she said to me the following morning, when after breakfast she appeared in her neat coat and skirt, with hat and gloves, ready to go out, "so on the whole I think I will begin with a visit to the Haggetts."

"I may come with you, I suppose?" I suggested meekly.

"Oh, yes!" she rejoined carelessly.

Somehow I had an inkling that the carelessness of her mood was only on the surface. It was not likely that she—my sweet, womanly, ultra-feminine, beautiful lady—should feel callous on this absorbing subject.

We motored down to Bishopthorpe. It was bitterly cold, raw, damp, and foggy. The chauffeur had some difficulty in finding the cottage, the "home" of the imbecile gardener and his wife.

There was certainly not much look of home about the place. When, after much knocking at the door, Mrs Haggett finally opened it, we saw before us one of the most miserable, slatternly places I think I ever saw.

In reply to Lady Molly's somewhat curt inquiry, the woman said that Haggett was in bed, suffering from one of his "fits."

"That is a great pity," said my dear lady, rather unsympathetically, I thought, "for I must speak with him at once."

"What is it about?" asked the woman, sullenly. "I can take a message."

"I am afraid not," rejoined my lady. "I was asked to see Haggett personally."

"By whom, I'd like to know," she retorted, now almost insolently.

"I dare say you would. But you are wasting precious time. Hadn't you better help your husband on with his clothes? This lady and I will wait in the parlour."

After some hesitation the woman finally complied, looking very sulky the while.

We went into the miserable little room wherein not only grinding poverty but also untidiness and dirt were visible all round. We sat down on two of the cleanest-looking chairs, and waited whilst a colloquy in subdued voices went on in the room over our heads.

The colloquy, I may say, seemed to consist of agitated whispers on one part and wailing complaints on the other; this was followed presently by some thuds and much shuffling, and presently Haggett, looking uncared-for, dirty, and unkempt, entered the parlour, followed by his wife.

He came forward, dragging his ill-shod feet and pulling nervously at his forelock.

"Ah!" said my lady kindly, "I'm glad to see you down, Haggett, though I am afraid I haven't very good news for you."

"Yes, miss!" murmured the man, obviously not quite comprehending what was said to him.

"I represent the workhouse authorities," continued Lady Molly, "and I thought we could arrange for you and your wife to come into the Union tonight, perhaps."

"The Union?" here interposed the woman, roughly. "What do you mean? We ain't going to the Union?"

"Well! but since you are not staying here," rejoined my lady, blandly, "you will find it impossible to get another situation for your husband in his present mental condition."

"Miss Ceely won't give us the go-by," she retorted defiantly.

"She might wish to carry out her late father's intentions," said Lady Molly with seeming carelessness.

"The Major was a cruel, cantankerous brute," shouted the woman with unpremeditated violence. "Haggett had served him faithfully for twelve years, and—"

She checked herself abruptly, and cast one of her quick, furtive glances at Lady Molly.

Her silence now had become as significant as her outburst of rage, and it was Lady Molly who concluded the phrase for her.

"And yet he dismissed him without warning," she said calmly.

"Who told you that?" retorted the woman.

"The same people, no doubt, who declare that you and Haggett had a grudge against the Major for this dismissal."

"That's a lie," asserted Mrs Haggett doggedly; "we gave information about Mr Smethick having killed the Major because—"

"Ah," interrupted Lady Molly, quickly, "but then Mr Smethick did not murder Major Ceely, and your information therefore was useless!"

"Then who killed the Major, I should like to know?"

Her manner was arrogant, coarse, and extremely unpleasant. I marvelled why my dear lady put up with it, and what was going on in that busy brain of hers. She looked quite urbane and smiling, whilst I wondered what in the world she meant by this story of the workhouse and the dismissal of Haggett.

"Ah, that's what none of us know!" she now said lightly; "some folks say it was your husband."

"They lie!" she retorted quickly. The imbecile, evidently not understanding the drift of the conversation, was mechanically stroking his red mop and looking helplessly all round him.

"He was home before the cries of 'Murder!' were heard in the house," continued Mrs Haggett.

"How do you know?" asked Lady Molly quickly.

"How do I know?"

"Yes; you couldn't have heard the cries all the way to this cottage—why, it's over half a mile from the Hall!"

"He was home, I say," she repeated with dogged obstinacy.

"You sent him?"

"He didn't do it—"

"No one will believe you, especially when the knife is found."

"What knife?"

"His clasp-knife, with which he killed Major Ceely," said Lady Molly, quietly; "he has it in his hand now."

And with a sudden, wholly unexpected gesture she pointed to the imbecile, who in an aimless way had prowled round the room whilst this rapid colloquy was going on.

The purport of it all must in some sort of way have found an echo in his enfeebled brain. He wandered up to the dresser whereon lay the remnants of that morning's breakfast, together with some crockery and utensils.

In that same half-witted and irresponsible way he had picked up one of the knives and now was holding it out towards his wife, whilst a look of fear spread over his countenance.

"I can't do it, Annie, I can't—you'd better do it," he said.

There was dead silence in the little room. The woman Haggett stood as if turned to stone. Ignorant and superstitious as she was, I suppose that the situation had laid hold of her nerves, and that she felt that the finger of a relentless Fate was even now being pointed at her.

The imbecile was shuffling forward, closer and closer to his wife, still holding out the knife towards her and murmuring brokenly:

"I can't do it. You'd better, Annie—you'd better—"

He was close to her now, and all at once her rigidity and nerve-strain gave way; she gave a hoarse cry, and, snatching the knife from the poor wretch, she rushed at him ready to strike.

Lady Molly and I were both young, active, and strong, and there was nothing of the squeamish *grande dame* about my dear lady when quick action was needed. But even then we had some difficulty in dragging Annie Haggett away from her miserable husband. Blinded with fury, she was ready to kill the man who had betrayed her. Finally we succeeded in wresting the knife from her.

You may be sure that it required some pluck after that to sit down again quietly and to remain in the same room with this woman, who already had one crime upon her conscience, and with this weird, half-witted creature who kept on murmuring pitiably:

"You'd better do it, Annie—"

Well, you've read the account of the case, so you know what followed. Lady Molly did not move from that room until she had obtained the woman's full confession. All she did for her own protection was to order me to open the window and to blow the police whistle which she handed me. The police-station fortunately was not very far, and sound carried in the frosty air.

She admitted to me afterwards that it had been foolish perhaps not to have brought Etty or Danvers with her, but she was supremely anxious not to put the woman on the alert from the very start, hence her circumlocutory speeches anent the workhouse and Haggett's probable dismissal.

That the woman had had some connection with the crime Lady Molly, with her keen intuition, had always felt; but as there was no witness to the murder itself, and all circumstantial evidence was dead against young Smethick, there was only one chance of successful discovery, and that was the murderer's own confession.

If you think over the interview between my dear lady and the Haggetts on that memorable morning, you will realize how admirably Lady Molly had led up to the weird finish. She would not speak to the woman unless Haggett was present, and she felt sure that as soon as the subject of the murder cropped up the imbecile would either do or say something that would reveal the truth.

Mechanically, when Major Ceely's name was mentioned, he had taken up the knife. The whole scene recurred to his tottering mind. That the Major had summarily dismissed him recently was one of those bold guesses which Lady Molly was wont to make.

That Haggett had been merely egged on by his wife, and had been too terrified at the last to do the deed himself, was no surprise to her, and hardly one to me, whilst the fact that the woman ultimately wreaked her own passionate revenge upon the unfortunate Major was hardly to be wondered at, in the face of her own coarse and elemental personality.

Cowed by the quickness of events and by the appearance of Danvers and Etty on the scene, she finally made full confession.

She was maddened by the Major's brutality, when with rough, cruel words he suddenly turned her husband adrift, refusing to give him further employment. She herself had great ascendancy over the imbecile, and had drilled him into a part of hate and of revenge At first he had seemed ready and willing to obey. It was arranged that he was to watch on the terrace every night until such time as an alarm of the recurrence of the cattle-maiming outrages should lure the Major out alone.

This effectually occurred on Christmas morning, but not before Haggett, frightened and pusillanimous, was ready to flee rather than to accomplish the villainous deed. But Annie Haggett, guessing perhaps that he would shrink from the crime at the last, had also kept watch every night. Picture the prospective murderer watching and being watched!

When Haggett came across his wife he deputed her to do the deed herself.

I suppose that either terror of discovery or merely desire for the promised reward had caused the woman to fasten the crime on another.

The finding of the ring by Haggett was the beginning of that cruel thought which, but for my dear lady's marvellous powers, would indeed have sent a brave young man to the gallows.

Ah, you wish to know if Margaret Ceely is married? No! Captain Glynne cried off. What suspicions crossed his mind I cannot say; but he never proposed to Margaret, and now she is in Australia—staying with an aunt, I think—and she has sold Clevere Hall.

BY THE SWORD

Selwyn Jepson

Selwyn Jepson (1899–1989) was a member of a distinguished literary family. His father, Edgar, was a popular novelist who occasionally wrote crime fiction, and who became a founder member of the Detection Club, while his niece is Fay Weldon. Selwyn was educated at St Paul's School and the Sorbonne, and after serving in the First World War, he too became a novelist, producing books such as *The Red-Haired Girl* and *The Death Gong* during the Twenties. As a screenwriter in the Thirties, his credits included *The Riverside Murder*, loosely based on *Six Dead Men*, an excellent novel by the Belgian author S.A. Steeman, and *The Scarab Murder Case*, a 1936 film based on a Philo Vance mystery written by the American S.S. Van Dine.

During the Second World War, he worked for the Special Operations Executive, and for dangerous missions he often recruited women, in the face of fierce opposition, because he reckoned that they had "a far greater capacity for cool and lonely courage than men". This belief may have led him to create Eve Gill, his most successful series character. Eve's most memorable adventure was recorded in *Man Running*, a 1948 thriller which Hitchcock adapted a couple of years later as *Stage Fright*, with a cast including Jane Wyman, Marlene Dietrich, and Richard Todd. Jepson was a talented, unpretentious storyteller, as 'By the Sword', one of his early stories, demonstrates; it appeared in *Cassell's Magazine* in December 1930.

ALFRED CAITHNESS STAYED ON FOR CHRISTMAS FOR TWO reasons, quite apart from the cold weather, which he found easier to support at Dingle House than alone in his Baker Street flat. Snow had fallen heavily in the middle of the month and again on Christmas Day. It lay thickly now, with the thermometer showing four degrees of frost, and it hid the lawns of the Dingle gardens and coated the roofs and gables of the old house like icing sugar on a cake.

Although he told himself that the reasons he had stayed were because an old-fashioned Christmas appealed to him and also because his cousin Herbert would undoubtedly lend him two thousand pounds if he handled him right, there was another thing which kept him here.

This, however, he had not yet fully admitted to himself. He only knew that he was in no great hurry to talk to Herbert about the money.

Life was very pleasant at Dingle House, he reflected. Why go out of the way to speed one's own departure?

This morning he sat by the blazing logs in the great stone fireplace of the library and watched Barbara, who was his cousin's wife, sewing at some pink thing which lay like a pool of silken foam in her lap.

The boy, young Robert, who was five and a bit, was marching a regiment of tin soldiers up and down the low, broad window-sill behind her. Every now and then she would turn her head to smile at him and admire some new arrangement of their ranks. Lifeguards on horseback they were, with red coats and silver breast-plates, a gay and gallant company.

"You couldn't have given him anything he would have liked better, Alfred," she said. "It's the Caithness in him."

He nodded, but was more attentive to the graceful poise of her head on the white column of her neck.

"He'll be a soldier like the rest of them," she added, and sighed.

Her husband was not one, but only because his left leg was two inches shorter than his right, a childhood accident. Alfred, too, was an exception to the family tradition.

"I never cottoned to the idea," he remarked, following her thought, "but not because the old story frightened me."

"You mean that a Caithness always dies by the sword?"

She had been thinking of it a moment before, when she had seen Robert grown to a man and pursuing the career which his ancestors had fulfilled so gloriously.

"It's very queer, though," Alfred said, "how many of them have been killed that way."

He glanced at the crest carved in the limestone of the mantel-piece, a short sword gripped in a mailed hand.

"But in these days soldiering isn't so fashionable," he added. "Perhaps your boy will be a legal luminary like his famous father."

His eyes went back to her, to the helmet of sleek, fair hair and the cream of her temples.

Heaven! How sorry he was for her! Married to Herbert, who was twenty-eight years her senior. A lame, dry-voiced man, con-sciously enigmatical, proud of his keen logical brain, his freedom from sentiment and the cloying dangers of emotionalism. In other words, the Honourable Mr Justice Caithness, whose judgments in the criminal court were renowned for the clarity of their law and the severity of their consequences.

Small wonder his life was so often threatened! To hear the smug self-righteousness of the man's voice as he condemned some poor devil to penal servitude was enough to arouse any vengeance. If he had had one threatening letter since the last sessions, he must have had a dozen.

Alfred shifted restlessly in his armchair and banged the dottle out of his pipe against the hearth.

What joy could Barbara get out of a husband like that? Precious little. Where was he now, for that matter? Shut away in his study at the other end of the house with his dictionaries, encyclopædias and books of reference, striving to solve Torquemada's crossword puzzle by Wednesday night! That was his weekly excitement, his one relaxation from the administration of justice and the text-book, *Anomalies in Criminal Law*, which he was preparing with young Donaldson's help. (At the thought of Jim Donaldson, Alfred frowned.)

"Left—right—left—right—left!" sang Robert at the window.

"Barbara!" said Alfred, and stopped abruptly.

She looked up and then dropped her eyes quickly. He bit on the empty pipe.

"They are horsemen, dear," she explained, turning to the boy. "Only foot-soldiers march in step."

"These are diff'rent."

Alfred knew suddenly why he had stayed at Dingle House for Christmas. He went over to Robert and asked him to run along. The boy did not want to. A little disgruntled, he obeyed.

"I'll find the book of engines for Uncle Jim. An' I'll come back presently," he said at the door.

Alfred closed it on him and crossed to the chair in which the golden head was bent over the silk. She had not commented on his sending the child away and he took heart. Surely she guessed what was coming?

"I've been here ten days now," he said, searching for words, "and I've seen how things are—with you and Herbert."

"Alfred, please—"

But he hurried on. He knew what he wanted to say.

"You can't go on with it! You can't! You're sacrificing your life to an existence in which there is nothing but the dry dust of—of senility to warm your heart. He married you when you were too young to know anything about life. I saw it—I knew you in those days, remember. Your self-seeking, ambitious mother pushed you into his arms when you were little more than a child, because he was a rich and eminent man. Barbara, you are miserably unhappy, tortured, tied to a complacent fossil of a human being who has no more idea of love than—than that piece of wood!"

She had risen and was facing him with harassed eyes. He strode round the chair and tried to take her hands, but she snatched them behind her.

"Look at it honestly, Barbara! You know I'm stating no more than the truth of the thing. I've got eyes in my head. I've seen you looking at him, heard your silence when he says something particularly inane. You're rushing into disaster. Presently you'll begin to look for an escape and, because the desire is so urgent, your judgment will be faulty. You'll make a ghastly mistake. Some casual man will take advantage of your misery—"

"Alfred, stop!"

"I won't stop. You've got to listen to me. I've loved you from the moment I first saw you, in that church at Herbert's side. Loved you, Barbara, d'you hear? I have the right to talk to you like this. I have the right to look after you—to take you away."

She stared at him with her hands to her cheeks, as though she could not believe what she heard. Dared not, Alfred thought with a throb of triumph. The words came easily now.

"You must come away with me—you and the boy. You won't have to give him up. I wouldn't ask that. I can't take you to a luxurious home but I can give you the warmer things of life, of the heart. Listen, Barbara. You know how I have felt about you for a long time. Last summer when I was here, do you remember the harvesting, when we rode home in the dusk on the top of that great mound of hay? You guessed then, didn't you, my darling? I held back because I wasn't sure of you, because I hadn't realized quite how terribly unhappy you were. You put up a fine show and it deceived me. But this last week has been different. You haven't succeeded for a second in making me think you care at all for Herbert. How could you pretend? He—"

She shivered and broke into the spate of his sentences with low, broken phrases.

"Even if I don't care for him—even if I don't—does that give you the right to...? Alfred, he's my husband—and your cousin. I—I am loyal to him and you must be."

"Heaven!" he cried. "What does *he* matter beside you? It's *your* life—all the years of life and adventure and *being*—in front of you that count! Barbara!"

He moved closer to her, with his arms open to take her.

"You don't understand—"

Then the door-handle creaked and he stopped, drew away. Jim Donaldson came in, his broad figure filling the doorway and his wide-set blue eyes cheerfully alert.

"Oh, hullo," he said, and strolled into the room. If he saw Alfred's scowl he ignored it. If he noticed the white, strained face of Barbara Caithness, he showed no sign.

"Cigarettes about?" he asked and stretched his shoulders, for he had been writing solidly since ten. Alfred disliked him cordially. The crispness of his speech, the health and honesty of his eyes, were irritating. This was the sort of man he saw as a danger to Barbara, living under the same roof with her when she was in this state of mind.

He saw the effort with which she picked up her sewing and made pretence of an easy mind. It was the gallant spirit he so admired in her, that, and all the perfection of form and feature which was hers. A woman in a million... his woman. Thank heaven he had had the courage to tell her so. It had startled her a bit but in a little she would see the thing more clearly. Damn this fellow Donaldson. Couldn't the oaf see they were wanting to talk to one another? He watched him take possession of an armchair and thrust his feet toward the fire.

"No sign of the thermometer letting up. But it's going to stay bright, thank goodness."

But he wasn't as dull as he seemed. Alfred saw his quick glance at the girl. She wasn't giving anything away, though.

Just as well, although the world would soon know about it. Herbert last of all—and not before they had gone. It would be a blow to the man's pride, but undoubtedly good for him to discover a flaw in his omnipotence.

Donaldson, who could not be told to "run along," looked as though he proposed to sit there until lunch-time. Alfred searched for some excuse to get rid of him or a cue that would enable Barbara to come outside, but unsuccessfully.

The boy returned at this point, burdened with a picture book and determined to engage Uncle Jim's attention. The library seemed crowded and Alfred left it in ill-humour. He wanted to think. The situation had developed almost by itself. He did not find himself surprised now that it had come at last and he had put words to it, but he was aware of a kind of breathlessness. Emotion, of course, and largely a physical one. He was quite experienced enough to realize that.

He went through the lounge toward the wide stairs.

As his footsteps died away, Donaldson sat up straightly in his chair, all his carelessness gone. In its place was anxiety and concern.

"It has come, has it?"

"I'm frightened of him, Jim. I tried to stop him—"

"—but he ranted on. I know. Oh, damn. Why didn't I arrive a bit earlier? Had it been going on long?"

Her distress cut his heart.

"No. But he said dreadful things about—Herbert. He blamed him and—"

"He would. He's jealous, you see, of all that Herbert has which he hasn't. Money—success—fame. That's why he wants you. To have you, to steal you—make you follow him—would convince him of his own power. Power he knows in his heart of hearts, he can never achieve. But you needn't worry. You mustn't! Just yell for me if he starts again."

"It's difficult, Jim. You see, he knows. I don't mean about you and me, but about my not being happy."

He went to her and touched her hand, while Robert, realizing with the infallible instinct of his age that his elders were more interested in themselves than in him, went back to his Lifeguards on the window-sill.

Donaldson spoke softly, with gentleness.

"Was it only yesterday we discovered one another? I'm still a little dazed but I'm beginning to think straight. My dear, I shall have to tell Herbert, and go. It's the only thing to do. I'll tell him soon. To-morrow. I shan't involve you. He'll be fair. You know, sometimes I think he knows already—and understands. That he knew before I myself did. He's odd in that way. More intuitive and sympathetic than people realize."

She nodded slowly, and her eyes shone mistily as she looked at him.

"Beloved," he said, "I shall carry you in my heart to the end of my days."

They lunched, the four of them, at the refectory table in the dining-room. A pewter bowl of holly in the middle partially hid husband and wife from one another, and Donaldson from Alfred. But Jim had no need to see Alfred's face to sense his triumph. He realized that the man's conceit, born of unconscious inferiority, would never permit him to see that Barbara, far from being pleased by his declaration, had indeed been nauseated and frightened by it.

She had always vaguely despised Alfred, not necessarily because he seemed constitutionally unable to keep any job more than three months, but because it was never, by the remotest chance, his fault that he lost it. "I told 'em to go to blazes," or: "I've got my principles and when a firm does *that* sort of thing—well, I leave them to it." Then, complaining bitterly that the gods seemed to have picked on him as their perpetual scapegoat, he would "borrow" some more money from Herbert to carry on with until something turned up.

Sometimes, too, he had said things about women, which in a queer way made one squirm. But for a certain charm, an indefinable quality, which made him an excellent companion when the mood was upon him, she could have hated him thoroughly. She was near to it now. He was complicating things for her at a difficult moment in her life. She was glad Jim was going to confess to Herbert. She would like to be there and face it with him. She loved, and was neither ashamed nor afraid. But Jim was right. He must leave her.

Lunch came to an end and she went up to her room to lie down and escape Alfred. Jim set off for a tramp across the Downs, taking the spaniels. He wanted to think out the future and nerve himself for the ordeal of saying good-bye to Barbara. Life had got to be lived somehow. Whatever happened he must not be long alone with her.

Alfred was also of a mind to consider the future and the practical aspect of the money shortage in view of his decision to take Barbara away now became very clear to him. He must settle it as soon as possible. With the thought of Barbara strengthening his resolve, he followed the limping Herbert from the lunch table to the study.

His spirits were high and a feeling of invincibility stimulated him. Herbert would stump up like a gentleman. He was as certain of it as he had been of anything in his life.

He accepted a cigar and hoped, he said, that he wasn't in the way.

"How's the book going?"

"Very well, Alfred. Donaldson's help is invaluable. An exceedingly astute brain for such a young man. His knowledge of jurisprudence is remarkable. He'll make a great name for himself when he begins practising in earnest. Like few men with large private incomes, he is ambitious. He will be Attorney-General before he has finished."

"Lucky devil," Alfred commented. "I wish I had had a quarter of his chances. I'm only a couple of years older than he is and, if things had been a bit different—gone better for me—I would be doing as well. It's not a comfortable feeling, that."

Herbert put on a pair of spectacles and turned over a page in a dictionary.

"You indeed seem to have been unfortunate," he said.

Alfred nodded and glanced at his cousin. The keen, straight face was not unsympathetic. This seemed to be the moment.

"I've been on the wrong tack, that's the whole trouble," he went on. 'I've always been doing things for other people instead of for myself. Look at that Sugar Beet Exploitation business! Why, in six weeks I'd put the thing on its feet! I suppose I did more to start that company off than anybody else in it. It must have made a profit of a hundred thousand this year. You see if I'm not right when they publish the balance sheet next month! And I would have been on the board but for Murgatroyd. I made a friend of the man and he started some ridiculous gossip about a row I had had in Coventry with the Invicto crowd. He had got it all wrong, of course, but that didn't prevent people listening to him. It got round to me in time, thank goodness. I called him a scandal-mongering liar to his face and walked out. They tried to get me back, of course, but I wouldn't go.

"No, the whole secret of it is that I ought to be my own boss. Herbert, I've got the idea of a lifetime. An export agency business. A one-man business. And with this new fiscal policy gaining ground all the time I'm on to a marvellous thing. New markets will be open-ing up every day and there's scarcely a firm or organization in this country ready to put home manufacturers in touch with the fresh fields. I could do it and ship their stuff for them on a commission basis—quite a small one. There's a fortune in it!"

"It sounds quite an idea," said Herbert.

"Lord, I should think it is! But the devil of it is, it will cost money to get it going."

"These things do."

"At least a couple of thousand pounds."

"Yes?"

"Of course I shall be able to pay it back out of profits in a year—two years."

Herbert nodded, closed the dictionary and inspected his cigar.

"I'm afraid I shan't be able to help you very much," he said.

Alfred's eyes moved uneasily. Well, perhaps two thousand was rather a lot all at once.

"I might manage it with fifteen hundred—" he leaned forward. "It's a great opportunity from the investment point of view. At a most conservative estimate, the man who puts up the capital would see twenty or twenty-five per cent return per annum. I've worked it out, you see."

Herbert was silent.

"You said yourself that the idea was a good one," Alfred pointed out. "Frankly, Herbert, I was counting on you to see the—"

Herbert had taken a small notebook out of a drawer in his desk and Alfred paused uncertainly. What was the fool doing now?

"In the last eight years, Alfred," he heard him saying, in a quiet, unemotional tone. "I have lent you six thousand pounds. I say 'lent,' because on each occasion that you have appealed to me you have spoken of repayment. I do not for a moment suggest that you have deliberately borrowed from me without intention of paying me back, but neither do I pretend to you that I regard these sums as anything but gifts. Indeed, they appear in this record under the heading of *Monies Given to A.C.* I have been very glad to help you and I am making no criticism. But, if I am not mistaken, I made a point of telling you when we discussed the matter on the fifteenth of July last that I would be unable to continue these—ah—loans."

"Yes, but Herbert, this is—"

"Different, I think you wish to say? I am sorry, but I am unable to detect in this any intrinsic variation from your previous applications. I regret it exceedingly, Alfred, but, quite definitely and finally, no! I feel, and have felt for some while, that if you are ever to be successful it must be based on your own, unaided efforts. To continue to give you money—I put it bluntly, I am afraid—can only serve to postpone your chance of doing something worth while."

"All right," Alfred interrupted. "I quite understand. We'll say no more about it. As to the six thousand I've already had, I said I would repay it and I will."

His voice was quiet. It surprised and had an effect on his cousin, who seemed a little less sure of himself, almost as though he doubted momentarily the wisdom of his course. But his mouth tightened and Alfred, watching him narrowly, knew all hope had gone.

He rose and put half an inch of cigar ash carefully in the ashtray on the edge of the desk.

"You're a stubborn old thing, Herbert, but don't worry your head about me. I'll manage, I dare say."

He went out, and closed the door gently.

He did not immediately proceed on his way, however, but stood tensely in the corridor fighting the weakness which attacked his limbs. He told himself that he was calm, unperturbed by the catastrophe of that blank refusal. He should have foreseen its suddenness and now remain untroubled by its significance. Laugh! Show that you don't care a damn!

But he whispered a little thickly: "Turned down! The swine turned me down!"

He walked unsteadily along the corridor with his mind confused by a swirl of thoughts. Barbara... the money... Herbert's stern face, with its eyes full of comprehension hovering in front of him.

His fingers closed tightly. Herbert had everything, hadn't he? All the money. The fate of men in his hands. The fate of Alfred Caithness, also. Even of Barbara. And by what right? By what right of God or man? The pale limping devil!

Then, before he reached the end of the corridor, an idea came which banished the shadows of uncertainty as with a bright light.

He stopped and became quite still, holding his breath as though he feared some eavesdropper of his mind.

He would kill Herbert. The money would come to Barbara.

Kill him, but not in this passion of hatred which possessed him now. Kill him quietly, unseen. Kill him in the night, secretly, so that no one could tell by whose hand he had died. The life of the Honourable Mr Justice Caithness had been threatened by many men who believed that he might have punished their sins less savagely. There had been comments in the Press about it and, a little while ago, after the Glastonbury blackmail case, a police guard had been put to watch over him until the fuss quietened down.

The money would come to Barbara.

As the thought took shape and became decision, he realized that only through the death of this man would his own life, so long buried in a morass of inhibition and failure, grow and blossom to fruitfulness.

Barbara, free at last, could come openly to his arms after a little while.

Thank Heaven he had not quarrelled with Herbert just now! Some blessed instinct must have warned him. An omen of success.

He began to think, to plan, and found himself curiously clear-headed and tranquil. The impatience was there and the need to give expression to this dominant desire which had been born in him. But these, far from hampering him, stimulated and enlivened his imagination.

He lay down on the divan in the library and closed his eyes.

First and foremost, he must school himself to appear normal when the others appeared. He must keep from his eyes and voice the excitement of his heart. There must be nothing they could remember afterwards and hold against him when the inquiry came.

Next, it must be a simple crime. The act of a man who is seeking vengeance without much thought for the consequences. An unsubtle, rather brutal murder...

His glance fell on the long Elizabethan dagger hanging with other antique arms on the wall between the windows. He did not get up and inspect it more closely, but he remembered handling it idly years ago. A weighty, dangerous weapon.

It would come readily to the hand of anyone who climbed in by one of the windows. These were very low to the ground. He saw the carpet of snow stretching across the tennis lawn to the drive and the London road. The road itself had been cleared and threaded like a black ribbon between the white hills.

He drew a sudden deep breath, like a swimmer who comes out of the buffeting of heavy waves into smooth water.

At tea he was quiet. This suited both his mood and his tactics. Barbara would expect him to be on tenterhooks because of his declaration this morning. Herbert, knowing him to be disappointed about the money, would not look to him for any great display of cheerfulness. He noticed that Donaldson was rather silent but that was no more than reasonable in a man who had walked nearly ten miles since lunch.

Barbara talked of little things, but with an effort. Alfred thought he knew why and was wrong. Only Donaldson knew.

She, like himself, was seeking the courage to face a grievous parting. They were both dreading and yet welcoming the morrow. Being near each other was heaven, but the agony of the situation was difficult to bear.

Herbert was the only one of them who seemed to be in an entirely normal frame of mind. He was amiable and discursive. He was glad Alfred had decided to be philosophical. There was no reason why he should not pull himself together and make good.

Dusk had fallen before five. By half-past it was almost dark, with the snow outside a vague blur of lightness.

At a quarter-to-seven the dressing-gong sounded and Alfred, once again in the library, heard the others go to their rooms. He had several minutes in which to work. With a little hurrying he could do what he had to do and be changed and in the drawing-room before the rest.

He went swiftly to the window he had chosen and, opening it, stepped carefully out into the snow. The closed curtains would hide him from the eyes of an unlikely invader of the room. He stood for a moment in the darkness and then ran silently in the yielding snow, covering the fifty yards across the lawn and down the drive to the road in less than half-a-minute. He then turned and *walked* back to the window, taking a slightly indirect route.

His reasoning was sound. The traces of a murderer who had come from outside would appear clearly in the snow between the road and the house but not on the road, which was clear.

Furthermore they would indicate that he had cautiously approached the scene of his intended crime and, having committed it, had fled quickly away.

In preparing this evidence he was at pains to make sure that the two sets of tracks did not intersect. Were they to do so, it might betray the fact that the running ones had been made before the walking ones. He was taking no chances. That the road was free from snow was a godsend. A car could have stood there, its wheel-marks lost in those of previous and later traffic, while the man was about his job. And, since the footprints passed in and out of the snow at nearly the same spot on the edge of the road, obviously, the detectives would say, a car had been used.

He regained the window, parted the curtains stealthily and stepped across the sill into the room. He closed the window and wiped what little frozen snow there was from the edges and soles of his boots, using a handkerchief which he dropped into the red heart of the fire as he passed it on his way to the door.

They were not his boots, but an old pair at least two sizes larger than his own which he had come upon some nights ago, when he was looking for an extra blanket, at the bottom of a cupboard on the landing outside his bedroom.

He reached his room unseen and, while the boots were drying on the radiator, changed quickly into his dinner jacket. On the way down to the drawing-room he returned them unobserved to their place, confident that they would never be connected with the tracks in the snow and that, even if by some incredible chance they were, there would be no evidence to show that he had ever worn them.

He was reading in the drawing-room when the others came down. Donaldson was more himself and Herbert mellower than his wont. If Barbara was pale, the two younger men had their own and different explanations for it. Herbert, who seldom if ever betrayed his observation, seemed, however, not to have noticed it. He went to his study after dinner, but reappeared within a few minutes in the drawing-room and suggested Bridge.

It was a welcome suggestion and enabled those who heard it to get through what threatened for each of them to be a difficult evening.

The game came to an end after the fifth rubber at about half-past ten, with Alfred the only winner, twenty-seven shillings to the good.

"Luck seems to be in," he said. A few minutes later he asked Barbara to excuse him and bade them good night.

Herbert nodded very amiably to him as he went and Alfred interpreted a relief that he had made so little fuss. Selfish hypocrite!

He closed the door of his bedroom, got quickly into pyjamas and dressing-gown, lay down under the eiderdown and, switching off the light, composed himself to wait as patiently as he might.

The moment for action was approaching. Herbert, one of those people who seemed to need very little sleep, would follow his invariable custom of reading a book by the library fire for some while after the rest of the household had gone to bed.

Alfred listened to the sounds in the old house and analysed them as they occurred.

Once during this period he experienced a moment of uncertainty, which was when he heard Barbara pass his door on her way to her room. She stopped and went back to the landing. He thought he heard Donaldson's voice in a subdued key.

He smiled grimly. Was that brilliant young fellow already falling under her spell?

He heard her return after several minutes and noticed that she walked slowly. He resisted the strong impulse to open his door and speak to her, to see her alone for a moment or two and to hold her closely in his arms. The thought of her embrace made him tremble. Time enough in the swiftly-approaching future. Time enough.

She went into her room and the door closed. Donaldson's was too far away in the east wing to be heard, but Alfred detected his heavy tread on the polished oak as he crossed the landing into the passage which led to it.

What had they said to one another? It was an idle, vaguely jealous question. But he comforted himself with the knowledge that, if Donaldson was beginning to get tiresome, he could soon be dealt with when matters had been straightened out. Barbara was too attractive to be allowed any great degree of freedom. When Herbert was out of it, and she—

He forced his attention to the necessities of the present and, after lying there for twenty minutes or so, swung his feet off the bed into a pair of felt-soled slippers.

He made no sound on the stairs and his movements across the darkened lounge towards the library door were no less silent. The thin line of light beneath it reassured him.

He opened it quietly, but without stealth, and closed it without undue noise.

Herbert, stretched out in an armchair with his shoes off looked up from his reading and peered out of the restricted radiance of the reading-lamp on the small table by his side, the only light in the big room.

"It's I—Alfred. I forgot to look out a book before I went up."

He came within the radiance of light, his hands comfortably in his dressing-gown pockets, as casual a figure of a man as could be imagined.

Herbert eyed him keenly for a moment, seemed about to say something, changed his mind, and remarked:

"You read *An Experiment in Time*, didn't you? Try the third shelf over there, behind the chesterfield. Most of the newer books are there."

"Thanks."

Herbert returned to his book after a moment and Alfred moved to the shelf suggested. He was aware of an immense and stifling excitement. He glanced at the rows of books, but without seeing them. He strolled along the shelves, with his back to the man in the chair. He came close to the corner and the windows between which the Elizabethan poinard hung.

He concentrated on a title in front of him. Read it aloud.

"*Life of Machiavelli*, by Villari," he said. "Any good?"

"A little solid. The Victorian biographical fashion." Herbert did not look round.

"H'm."

Alfred thought, "Machiavelli, the man of cunning and ingenuity."

Machiavelli—Machiavelli—The name ran in and out of his brain like a rat scampering in a bundle of hay. Keep still! Keep quiet!

He edged silently to the wall between the windows and lifted down the dagger. His mind slowed and became rational. Only his breathing was a little faster than normal as his grip closed round the hilt.

Murder in theory was now to be murder in fact. For a moment he had to nerve himself for the physical necessity of action. No holding back now!

The back of Herbert's head was visible above the chair. He was deeply engrossed. Alfred's four paces across the strip of carpet which lay between the windows and the fireplace were quite noise-less and Herbert gave no sign of even a subconscious perception of the movement behind him.

But suddenly he spoke.

Alfred, with a tremor of anxiety, came to an abrupt stop within three feet of him, the dagger held out of sight. Then he realized, by the pitch of Herbert's voice, that he thought he was still at the other side of the room. In relief he stepped swiftly backwards to the shelves again.

"What's that?" he asked.

"I said: 'Did you get my note?'"

Alfred brought his wits together with an effort.

"Note?"

"I put it on your dressing-table after dinner, before we started Bridge. Never mind. You must have overlooked it." He glanced round and added: "Read it when you go up again. And before we close the subject finally, let me impress upon you that I mean every word of it."

Alfred was glad that he turned back to his book at that moment. He could not believe that his own quivering emotion, a mingling of rage and nervousness which he controlled with every particle of will he possessed, did not show in his face.

"I see," he said, and felt sure that the thickness of his tone was perceptible. "I'll remember. Yes. I must have overlooked it. I'll read it when I go up."

Written evidence that there had been trouble about money between them! Lying about on a dressing-table! That letter must be destroyed the moment he got back to his room. Destroyed beyond all tracing. He knew perfectly well what was in it. Typical of Mr Justice Caithness! A categorical restatement in writing of his refusal to give his unsatisfactory cousin another penny! "And let me impress upon you that I mean every word of it!"

All right! Savour your power! Savour it well while you have it, cousin Herbert! For you won't have it long!

Alfred moved again across the space of carpet, his mouth like a scar which is nearly healed, thin and mauve with the tenseness of his muscles. He was no longer conscious of hesitation, of physical reluctance. Savage determination burned in him like a fire.

Herbert did not speak this time, attentive to his book. However, a fraction of a second before the knife swept sideways over the armchair, he straightened himself a little, as though some sixth sense had begun to stir, to warn him of the peril which was upon him.

But the small movement availed him nothing. Indeed, it exposed his side and made the blow more certain.

Alfred used all his strength. Far more, actually, than was necessary to reach the heart, driving the slim blade under the ribs at a slightly upward angle.

He whipped back his hand and left the weapon there.

A slight gasp, it could scarcely be called an exclamation, was the only sound with which Death came. The body twisted once and was still. The head lolled down on to the white shirt front.

Alfred stood motionless behind the chair for perhaps three age-long seconds and then held out his hand in the white rays from the reading-lamp and stared at it. It was quite steady.

He looked up and saw the Caithness crest carved in the stone. It glowed redly in the firelight.

Funny. Even Herbert, lame and sedentary all his days, had come to his end by the sword. The aptness of it pleased strangely.

He took the white handkerchief from the dead man's breast pocket and, bending down, rubbed the hilt of the dagger clean of possible finger-prints. He arranged the handkerchief neatly in its pocket again and went to the window.

Kneeling on the wide sill, the curtains closed behind him, he took out a penknife, opened the window with his hand wrapped in the skirt of his dressing-gown and scratched the paint-work of the frame where the latch came, so that it would look as though it had been forced from outside. The garden was dark and silent, and the cold of the snow smote his cheeks.

He shut the penknife and slipped it back into his dressing-gown pocket.

As he did so he heard a short sound in the room. An inexplicable clatter. It brought his breath to a standstill, cutting him to the depths of his being with sharp, agonizing fear.

He slid off the sill on to the floor behind the curtains, his one instinct being to keep low and out of sight. He landed on hands and knees, rather heavily, crouching and in great fright lest he was bulging the bottom of the curtains.

He stayed there, utterly still, with every sense alert to define the slightest noise or movement in the room he could not see.

As the persistent quietness, unbroken after that one sound, reassured him somewhat, he crawled backwards a foot or so, and put his eye to the join of the curtains.

The library was peaceful, and held nothing living. The dead man's legs and his dangling right arm broke the silhouette of the armchair before the fire. They had not moved.

He stole across the room and saw that the book Herbert had been reading had dropped from his knees to the floor and, striking the shaft of a steel poker as it fell, had disturbed it on the stone hearth.

He brushed his lips with a nervous hand and had the presence of mind to leave the light switched on. A man who fled in haste would not wait to turn it off.

He went unhurriedly out of the library.

All had gone according to plan. No one had heard him, no one had seen him.

As he passed through the lounge he was conscious of a smarting sensation in the top of his thumb and sucked it mechanically. He felt a piece of broken skin with his tongue and wondered vaguely how he had done it.

But he was thinking of the letter on the dressing table and the necessity for obliterating it. Burn it? Yes, in the wash-basin. Swill the ashes down the waste pipe. That would do it.

He reached his room and found the letter, lying under his evening-dress collar. Showed how intent he must have been when he was undressing, not to have noticed it.

He tore it open and read it. His hand shook.

Dear Alfred,

Here it is, but positively I will not be able to do this again. I believe that you honestly want to succeed in this new project and I detect in you a different attitude. I think it is a genuine one.

Good luck,

Herbert.

A slip of pink paper, a blue stamp in the corner... a cheque for two thousand pounds.

He stared at it like a man in a trance. The unexpectedness of the thing found him without the capacity for adjustment. His mind flickered helplessly like a candle in a wind and it was several moments before it gathered strength and direction.

Herbert had relented. Affection, generosity—heaven knew what—had moved him to alter his decision.

Herbert… whom he had killed.

He covered his eyes and swayed a little on his feet. What had he done?

He caught at his uncertain thoughts and strove to order them.

Then, with sudden uprising, resentment came to his aid.

The magnanimous prig! He had given the money, yes! But with a cramped spirit, reflecting that cramped soul!

He was glad he had killed him! *Glad!* He exulted in it.

And he had *not* killed him uselessly.

Had he been allowed to live there would still have remained the problem of Barbara. His death had set her free—free. Nothing stood between them now.

It had had to be. Fate had ordained that he should not see the letter until afterwards.

He would not dream of destroying it. Together with the cheque it removed beforehand any motive the authorities could find should they, by some impossible effort of imagination, suspect him.

He was safer than ever.

He regarded himself carefully in the mirror, and saw nothing in his eyes to suggest knowledge of what he had done, of what had happened downstairs.

He glanced at his wrist-watch. It congratulated him that he had been out of his bedroom exactly nine-and-a-half minutes.

He took off his dressing-gown and slid between the cold sheets.

But he did not sleep.

His deportment the next morning, during the hour of horror which followed the discovery of the murder by a housemaid, was precisely what it should have been. His pallor and shakiness were no more than to be expected. It was he who rang up the police station and, as a relative of the dead man, took upon his shoulders the burden of the affair in those respects which would have caused pain to Barbara.

He welcomed the Superintendent and the Detective-Inspector, and was exceedingly helpful to those individuals in their preliminary investigation. The tracks in the snow, the open window and the fact that Mr Justice Caithness had not infrequently received threatening letters of one kind or another, seemed to indicate the character and motive of the crime as clearly as any overworked policeman could desire.

"We'll get the fellow all right," said the Detective-Inspector and set about taking measurements and subjecting the library, the window and the snow to an inch by inch examination. The Superintendent departed to make inquiries in the neighbourhood for evidence of suspicious strangers.

Jim Donaldson seemed to be in a queer state, a profound silence. Only Barbara, in those moments when she could drag her mind from the numbness of shock, realized what he was feeling. Life had played him a trick. He had gained his heart's desire in the eleventh hour but he had paid for it dearly.

He saw her alone for a moment during that terrible morning, and said:

"I shall get over it, my dear, but I have an awful sensation, deep in me, that I have cheated somewhere, somehow."

She shook her head.

"*He* would not think so."

He took courage at that and saw the sun shining on the snow-burdened trees. Presently it would disappear, magically.

*

Alfred, grim but professedly interested in the Detective-Inspector's procedure, watched the man at work. He was satisfied that all was going well but he was not blind to the sudden abstraction which came upon the police officer shortly before mid-day.

He saw him find a finger-print, a single one, on the white paint of the window-sill and also (neither of them paid much attention to it at the moment) a toy soldier on the carpet just below it.

"One of young Robert's," Alfred explained. "He was playing with them here yesterday. He must have—"

He stopped.

The Detective-Inspector, who was puzzled by the fact that the print, which was so particularly clear except for an unevenness in the middle and looked like that of a left thumb should be alone in its glory, noticed the sudden pause.

He did not realize that his companion was struggling with a rising, an overwhelming panic, because he had seen that the tiny sword of the Lifeguardsman was bent and that something had dulled the brightness of its point.

"The sword—" he muttered and, with his forefinger, felt the small place on the pad of his left thumb where the skin was broken. "Oh my God! By the sword!"

The Detective-Inspector regarded him curiously and said nothing.

He was not unaccustomed to the sight of a guilty man's face.

It was in that moment that he neglected the trend of his inquiry for a less obvious one. And after a little things began to fit in… a very curious affair. And then the widow's story.

Counsel for the Defence did his best. He asked, was it sensible to suggest that a man should murder the person who had given him so many reasons for gratitude? Two thousand reasons, for example, that very evening?

But the jury thought it might be. Apart from all that, however, they were much impressed by the evidence of the finger-print expert and the doctor, who together were unshakeably convincing on the subject of the prisoner's left thumb. The blood-chemist proved very successfully that the print on the window-sill had not been there more than ten hours when the Inspector found it. The time it had been made corresponded with the time of the murder.

The prisoner displayed no great effort in denying the charge the Crown had brought against him. He listened to the proceedings without emotion, his eyes now and again fixing themselves in an unwavering stare on the smallest of the exhibits ranged on the table in the well of the court. A toy Lifeguard with a broken sword.

It seemed to fascinate him.

He was hanged in May.

THE CHRISTMAS CARD CRIME

Donald Stuart

Donald Stuart was one of the pen-names adopted by John Robert Stuart Pringle (1897–1980), a prolific writer whose work, especially under his principal pseudonym Gerald Verner, bore the influence of that great entertainer Edgar Wallace. Like Wallace, he had a flair for publicity, as an interview he gave to the *Surrey Comet* describing his rise from rags to riches makes clear. The journalist breathlessly recorded how "he once sat up all night and guarded the dead body of a man lest he should rise and frighten his timid wife—the wife was Mr Verner's landlady, and for his services he was absolved from the cost of board and living which he could not pay. He has 'bumped' ice at Billingsgate, designed posters and magazine covers, been a pavement artist, a journalist, produced cabarets for £200 a week, acted, associated with thieves and cut-throats, and done a hundred and one other exciting things… Now, at the age of 40, he is one of the most successful crime writers in the country… He has a huge public, one and a half million copies of his books having been sold, and he also has the distinction of having constituted what is probably a record output—23 novels in five years, as well as nearly 100 short stories, serials, and two film scenarios." Nor was that all: "A man of amazing memory and powers of concentration, he can write several books at once without losing the thread of any of them… and spends the little spare time he has motor boating on the Thames."

It is the customary fate of most such mass producers for their work to fall into neglect once they cease to market and publish their wares so energetically, and Stuart is, alas, no exception. However, the reason for the success he achieved was that he knew how to engage his readers, and this story is a good example of his talent to entertain. It first appeared in *Detective Weekly* No. 96, in December 1934.

W ITH A LONG HISS OF ESCAPING STEAM THAT SOUNDED like light relief the Western Express came to a halt beside the platform at Bodmin Station. From a first class compartment a tall, thin man alighted, and turned to assist a middle-aged lady, whose ample proportions were enveloped in a voluminous coat of some mysterious black, furry material.

"I hope there's a waiting room," she remarked, shivering violently as a blast of icy wind came whistling along the platform. "This weather is bad for them what's got rheumatics."

"I've no doubt there's a waiting room," said Trevor Lowe, the well-known dramatist, smiling at the woman's distortion of the King's English; "but we haven't very long to wait, anyhow. Our own train goes in twenty minutes."

He turned as his secretary Arnold White and Detective Inspector Shadgold joined them. "Will you see about the luggage?"

Arnold White nodded.

"We'll meet you at the train," added the dramatist. And as his secretary hurried away down the platform towards the guard's van: "Come along, Shadgold!"

The Scotland Yard man, his red face glowing, set his bowler hat more firmly on his bullet head, thrust his hands into the pockets of his overcoat, and fell into step at Lowe's side as they headed towards the bridge that crossed the line to the other platform.

The three of them were on their way to spend Christmas with a friend of Lowe's who lived at St Merryan, a little Cornish village nestling in the moors. The invitation was a long-standing one, and, if the truth must be told, the dramatist had forgotten all about it until his friend had written three days previously reminding him of his promise.

It had been Lowe's intention to spend Christmas at home, and he had invited Shadgold to join him. Reluctant to disappoint the burly inspector at the last moment, he had wired his friend, who was an old school chum, asking if he might bring the Scotland Yard man with him. The reply had been characteristic:

"Bring the entire police force, only come. I shall expect you on the 9.5, 23rd."

The journey from Paddington had been a long and tedious one, but the worst of it was over, and another couple of hours would see them at their destination.

They crossed the footbridge, found a waiting room, in which they installed the ample lady before a microscopic fire, as she waited for a different train, and went off to stretch their legs until the local train which would take them to St Merryan pulled in.

It was snowing heavily, and the platform beyond the shelter was covered with a thick layer of white which was gradually growing deeper.

"By Jove—it's cold!" grunted Shadgold, his ruddy face a deeper red and his breath steaming. "It's a treat to get a breath of fresh air, though, after the stuffiness of that carriage."

Lowe agreed. It was a tonic to breathe that ice-cold wind that had come across the snow-swept moor. They walked as far as the end of the shelter, and then turned to retrace their steps; and as they did so Lowe saw that the platform was no longer deserted. Several men were pacing up and down, and at the other end stood the solitary figure of a girl. They had obviously transferred from the Western Express, and were waiting to catch the 7.20 local.

Lowe was rather surprised that there should be so many passengers for this train, for it only ran to Tregoney, which was one station beyond St Merryan, and itself little more than a village. Almost mechanically he counted them. There were six men; the girl made the seventh passenger.

Arnold White accompanied by a porter with a loaded truck, joined them as they reached the foot of the steps leading up to the bridge, and Lowe dismissed the other people who were waiting for the train from his mind. Had he known what lay in store, and how important those seven passengers were to become, he would have taken more interest in them. But he had no knowledge then of the strange business in which he was to be involved, and the terrible experience which awaited him and his fellow travellers in the snow-flecked darkness of the night.

The train backed in to time. It was not a very long one, and there was only one first-class carriage. Lowe was hoping that they would have the compartment to themselves when the girl who had been waiting on the platform, and whom he had originally seen get into one of the other coaches, almost fell into the carriage.

She was breathing quickly, and as Lowe took her suitcase and put it on the rack he saw that she was trembling violently. Something had apparently frightened her, and he wondered what it was. With a murmured word of thanks she sat down in the corner seat which Arnold White gave up to her, and almost immediately became absorbed in a newspaper.

She was a slim girl, with a face that might have been lovely but for its extreme pallor. Lowe, who was watching her covertly, noticed that her stockings were of artificial silk. In the left one was a ladder that had been neatly darned, and her shoes were slightly down-at-heel. The gloves she wore were cheap, and two of the fingers had been carefully mended. Her coat was shabby, the fur at the neck worn, and the little black hat which was tilted on one side of the shapely head was obviously of the cheapest.

She looked up from the paper she was reading, and, catching Lowe's eye, looked down again quickly, but not before he had seen the startled expression which flashed for a moment in her grey eyes—an expression that held more than a percentage of fear.

With the preliminary blast of its whistle, the train began to move. It jolted forward, stopped, as though loath to leave the shelter of the station and face the coldness of the night, thought better of it, and with a resigned grunting started in earnest on its cross-country journey.

The girl did not look up again, but kept her eyes fixed on her paper, though Lowe was convinced that she was not reading. He began to feel curious about the girl, and amused himself by wondering who she was and where she was going. She had come from London, for he remembered having seen her on the platform at Paddington, and he concluded that most probably she was going home to her parents for Christmas. But why, and of what, was she afraid? He mused on this as the train thundered on, stopping every now and again at some small station to unload and take in parcels and mail. Most of these were only halts, and the last had been left some miles behind when the train, which had been gathering speed, suddenly slowed and, with a grinding of brakes, shuddered to a standstill.

"What are we stopping again for?" grunted Shadgold.

Trevor Lowe rubbed the misty glass of the carriage window with his coat-sleeve and peered out into the darkness.

"There's no sign of a station," he remarked. "There's no sign of anything that I can see except snow."

At that moment a flicker of light caught his eyes and he saw someone with a lantern hurry past the carriage. Presently there was a shout and a muffled sound of voices outside on the line. Lowering the window Lowe thrust out his head. The snow was falling thicker than ever, and he could see very little at first, but looking along the train he was able to make out in the lights from the carriage windows a group of men standing by the engine. Somebody shouted, and then Lowe saw the guard hurrying towards him carrying a lantern.

"What's happened?" he called, as the man came level with the carriage. "Why have we stopped?"

"Because we can't go on, sir," grunted the guard. "There's been a heavy fall of snow from the walls of the cutting ahead, and it's blocked the line."

"Does that mean we're stuck here indefinitely?" asked the dramatist.

"I'm afraid it does, sir," answered the railway official. "Till the morning, at any rate, perhaps longer, it all depends how long the breakdown gang will take to clear the snow away!"

Lowe turned back into the carriage to tell the others, while the guard passed on word of the trouble to other passengers.

"Well, rather than stay in the train all night, getting colder and colder," suggested Lowe, "I propose that we walk back along the line to the station we passed about twenty minutes ago. I should think we can bank on getting some sort of accommodation near the station, and anyway, it will be better to have a good walk than just to sit around hoping. What do you say?"

Arnold White and Shadgold agreed immediately. The rest of the travellers, when Lowe proceeded to sound them out, seemed only too willing to follow anybody who had a definite plan to do something.

As they set off on their curious midnight hike down the snow-covered permanent-way, Lowe looked round for the girl. Not seeing her in the little party he asked Shadgold what had happened to her.

"Well," said Shadgold, "I asked her to come with us, but she didn't seem to relish the idea of this walk; said she'd rather stop in the train and get some sleep. As a matter of fact, I don't think that coat of hers would have stood up against this cold wind. I would have offered her mine, but thought she might be offended…"

Lowe smiled in the darkness. The thought of that slender girl wrapped in the burly inspector's outsize in overcoats was a bit humorous, and Lowe could imagine, too, how awkward his friend Shadgold would have been in trying to play the gallant. Well, the girl was old enough to make up her mind and she was probably right to stay in the certain security of the train rather than face the uncertain prospects of the lonely countryside.

The group of stranded travellers soon got strung out in twos and threes. Lowe's group were last, chiefly because they elected to talk amongst themselves as they walked.

They had been making rather uneven progress for about a quarter of an hour, when from behind them came a thin shriek of terror. It was very faint, and could not have reached the next group in front. The three men halted in their tracks in an attitude of strained attention.

"Stay here, Shadgold, and alert the others what's happened," jerked Lowe. "White and I will run back and investigate."

With White at his heels he started to run back over their tracks, the whirling snowflakes buffeting his efforts to pierce the gloom ahead. Round a bend he was able to make out the vague, arched shadow of a bridge they had passed under some moments before. Then came another scream, which caused him and White to look up.

Dangling from a rope which hung from the parapet of the bridge was the figure of a girl. It was intuition rather than recognition which made Lowe associate that helpless figure instantly with the girl on the train. What had made her leave the train? Why on earth should anyone be trying to harm her? Though the question flashed through Lowe's mind he did not stop to work them out. Instead, he redoubled his speed and shouted to the vague figure on the bridge who was striving to haul the struggling girl to the top.

The effect of his shout was instantaneous—and drastic. The figure let go of his lasso, and the girl fell with a scream to the track. Luckily the snow helped break her fall, and beyond being winded and very frightened, she did not seem to be badly hurt.

Whilst Lowe assisted her to her feet and reassured her, White climbed the bank to the bridge in the hopes of getting a line on the mysterious assailant. But it was hopeless. The man, whoever he was, had a good start, and in the darkness and blinding snow it was futile trying to give pursuit. Lowe concurred when White slithered down to the track to report, so they turned back with the girl between them.

The girl was naturally frightened and shaking, but beyond saying that she could not make out at all why she should have been attacked, Lowe could get very little from her. He was sure she was keeping something back, but that, again, was her affair. He did ask her definitely why she had left the train after expressly stating to Shadgold that she would stay there.

"I would have stopped," she suddenly blurted, "but a man must have climbed up on to the footboard. I saw his face staring in... and... and it frightened me. I jumped out the other side and ran, meaning to catch up with you. He must have been waiting for me on that bridge."

It wasn't satisfactory enough to answer all the obvious queries that came to the dramatist's mind, but in view of the shock that she had suffered they forbore from pressing further questions.

When they rejoined Shadgold and the others, Lowe gave only the baldest outline of what had happened, nudging the inspector to save up his queries.

At length the party from the train reached the deserted station which had been their goal. Here, fresh disappointment awaited them. The place was an isolated halt, and the solitary railway official they found on duty quickly disillusioned them on their chances of finding any accommodation near Moorland Halt.

Glum and shivering, the little group stood on the snow-covered platform of Moorland Halt and stared in consternation at the solitary railway servant who covered the duties of porter, booking clerk and stationmaster.

"Do you mean to say," said Trevor Lowe, "that the nearest hotel is twelve miles away?"

"Ay, mister, I do," said the man. "Twelve mile it be, an' you can't stay 'ere because I'm goin' to lock up." He jerked his head towards the wooden shed at the end of the long platform, which constituted the entire station.

"Well, I think it's disgraceful!" declared an elderly, stoutish man. "Disgraceful! The railway company have got us into this position, and the railway company should get us out of it!"

"Since they're not likely to," remarked Lowe, "we must do something for ourselves."

The snow was still falling steadily, and to add to their discomfort the wind had risen, an icy, penetrating blast that swept across the open moorland and found its way through the thickest overcoat, chilling them to the marrow. The girl looked blue with cold, her threadbare coat offering little protection against that cutting north-easter.

"Surely there must be some place nearer than twelve miles," said Lowe irritably.

The porter shook his head impatiently.

"I tell you there ain't!" he answered. "Only the Chained Man, and you'd best stay out than go there."

"The Chained Man? What's that?" asked a tall, fair man, watching the shivering girl anxiously.

"It's a pub, about a mile away, along the Moor Road," replied the porter, "but if you takes my advice—"

"Why, what's the matter with the place?" asked the stout man.

"Well, it's queer," grunted the porter. "Joe Cornford, that's the landlord, is a surly brute, and the place ain't got too good a reputation. Nobody in these parts won't go near it. There was a feller killed there five years ago, and since then—"

"Never mind about it bein' queer, mate!" exclaimed the cockney. "I bet it's a darn sight better than freezing to death on this blinking platform."

"Oh, well, you please yourself!" said the porter, after a slight hesitation and shrugging his shoulders, "but I'd rather stay out on the open moor myself than spend a night at the Chained Man. If you come out of the station with me I'll show you the way."

They followed him to the wooden building that served as booking office and waiting room, waited while he carefully locked up behind him, and then descended a flight of wooden steps to the lower level of the road.

"Follow that there path," he said pointing to a ribbon of road that faded away in the curtain of falling snow. "And don't say I didn't warn yer. You'll find the Chained Man a mile along on the left."

They had some difficulty in keeping to the road, the thick covering of snow rendering it almost indistinguishable from the surrounding moorland. It seemed that they had walked miles and their feet and hands were numbed with the cold before a faint light ahead on the left of the road warned them that they had almost reached their destination.

As they drew nearer they heard the creaking of a signboard somewhere up in the snow-flecked darkness above them, and presently came upon the post that bore it. Away to their left was a shadowy building, from a first-floor window of which a light gleamed.

"Thank 'eaven!" said the little cockney fervently who during the walk, had confided to all and sundry that his name was Arty Willings. "Mother's wanderin' boy 'as come 'ome at last!"

Making his way up to the low porch Trevor Lowe found a rusted knocker and beat a thundering tattoo. There was a long delay and then the door was pulled open, and an unkempt, dirty-looking man holding an oil lamp peered out.

"What is it?" he growled ungraciously. "What do you want?"

Lowe rapidly explained the situation. The man, whom he took to be Joe Cornford, the landlord, nodded surlily.

"I can put you up," he said, "but you'll have to take pot luck. We ain't used to receiving guests 'ere these days."

"If you can provide us with a fire, something to eat and a decent bed, that's all we want," retorted Lowe.

"And some beer," put in Mr Willings. "Don't forget that, mate!"

"'Ow many of you are there?" growled the landlord.

"Ten," answered the dramatist.

"I've only got eight rooms," said Cornford, "but come in an' I'll do what I can."

They left their various suitcases in the passage and entered the room he indicated, an oblong, low-ceilinged apartment, with a fireplace at one end, in which they noticed, thankfully, a log fire was burning.

"Well, queer or not," remarked Mr Willings, warming his hands, "this is a blinking sight better than bein' out in the perishin' cold, ain't it?"

The stout man, who had confided to Lowe that his name was William Makepiece, heartily agreed with him.

The landlord returned with an armful of logs, and accompanied by a slatternly looking woman, whom he introduced as the "missus", and who said that she would show them the rooms. And unprepossessing enough they were—small, dirty and badly furnished. When they had washed in tepid water, brought them by the landlord, they went back to the coffee-room, to find the pleasant smell of fried bacon permeating the atmosphere and the table laid with a mixture of odd crockery.

During the meal that followed the dramatist took stock of his companions in misfortune. They were a curious, mixed lot, he found. There was William Makepiece—middle-aged, grey-haired, and jovial. The little dark-haired, ruddy-faced cockney,

Arty Willings. A pale-faced, thin man, who had as yet scarcely opened his lips, and whose name Lowe did not know. The young, fair-haired man, who had introduced himself as Frank Cotton, and who was paying marked attention to the girl. A bald-headed man, whose neatly waxed moustache was of a suspicious blackness; a little meek-faced man called Pilbeam, and the girl.

She interested Lowe more than any of them. The frightened look which he had surprised in her eyes when she had got in the carriage at Bodmin had deepened. He caught her once or twice glancing uneasily at the men grouped round the table. Her eyes flickered from face to face with an anxious, searching look, as though she was trying to satisfy herself about something that was troubling her mind. Did she recognize here the mysterious assailant on the bridge? Lowe had noticed something else. When he thought he was unobserved, the stout man, William Makepiece, kept on darting little covert glances at the girl. Lowe became aware of a curious tension in the atmosphere. He was unable to make up his mind from whence it emanated, but it was there, and it filled him with an unpleasant sense of unease.

When she had finished her meal the girl rose and with a muttered good-night left them, and, gathering round the fire, the rest of the party chatted desultorily until, by tacit consent, they broke up and made their way to their various rooms.

The wind had risen to a gale and was howling round the place, whistling in the chimneys and rattling the windows. Somewhere below a loose shutter was banging intermittently, and, tired though he was, this sound kept Lowe awake for some time. That peculiar feeling of unease that he had experienced in the coffee-room had become stronger and more potent. Instinct, which when fully

awake is stifled by reason, is more active when the brain is dulled
by the approach of sleep. Lying half-awake and half-asleep, the old
inn became, quite suddenly, sinister. The feeling that possessed
him was fanciful and imaginative, and he tried to throw it off,
but it persisted. As sleep took possession of his brain a picture
formed in his dreams, a picture of a frightened girl, crouching in
the middle of a circle of shadowy shapes—faceless shapes—who
mouthed and gibbered at her, and stretched out long, talon-like
hands to grasp her shrinking form. And then as she cried out in
her fear and terror, the faces suddenly took on form and features
and became the faces of the six men who had sat round the long
table in the coffee-room.

It seemed to Trevor Lowe that he had only been asleep for an
instant, when suddenly he was wide-awake. At first he thought it
was the sound of the loose shutter swinging in the wind that had
wakened him, and then, as he listened, he heard the low rumble of
voices. They came from somewhere beneath him, and he was on
the point of turning over and going to sleep again when he heard
somebody scream; a sharp cry of agony that broke off abruptly
in the middle!

He sat up in bed, his senses alert, but although he listened there
was now no sound from below. He slipped out of bed and put
on his jacket and trousers over his pyjamas and opened the door.

The passage was in pitch darkness, but when he reached the
head of the stairs he caught a momentary gleam of light from
the hall below.

"Who's there?" he called softly. "Anything the matter?"

Instantly the light went out, and he heard the creak of a door,
but no one answered.

He reached the hall and started to cross it to enter the coffee-room, but suddenly he stumbled and fell over something that lay on the floor. His hands, outstretched to check his fall, came in contact with something silky—silky and wet!

With a muttered exclamation he scrambled to his feet, opened the coffee-room door, and going over to the dying fire kicked one of the logs till it blazed. In the flickering light he examined his hands. They were both darkly stained with something that glistened red in the flame. A glance through the door and he discovered the reason.

Huddled on the floor was the figure of a man, clad in pyjamas and dressing-gown. Trevor Lowe went over and bent down. Staring up at him was the distorted face of the stout man, William Makepiece, and round the knife that protruded from the breast of his silk pyjamas was a similar stain to that which covered his hands.

The man was quite dead. One look at the sightless eyes staring up at the discoloured ceiling told him that. And it was murder!

He remembered the voices he had heard immediately on awakening, the sudden flash of light, and the creak of the door. On the end of the long table was the oil lamp, which the landlord had brought to the door to admit them. Lowe touched the china shade and drew his fingers away quickly. It was still unpleasantly hot. It must have been that light which he had seen when he called from the head of the stairs, and it must have been the murderer who had blown it out and escaped as Lowe made his way down to the hall.

An uncomfortable little shiver ran down his spine. The man must have been crouching somewhere in the darkness as he had groped his way to the door of the coffee-room…

He hurried over to the fireplace, and with a spill, which he made from a strip torn from an old newspaper, lighted the oil lamp. Then he bent down over the dead man, placing the lamp on the floor, so that its light shed a pool over the motionless form. The man had been stabbed through the left side of the chest, and the weapon was a large clasp knife with a horn handle. He saw something white gripped between the fingers; part of a large-sized Christmas card that had been torn across.

As he straightened up the figure of the landlord came in out of the gloom. He caught his breath as he saw Lowe, and then, as his eyes dropped to the thing on the floor, his coarse mouth fell open and he stared at it, his small eyes wide with horror.

"Did you kill him?" he whispered hoarsely, finding his voice.

"I? No!" snapped the dramatist. "I was awakened by a scream, and coming down I found him like this."

"Thunder!" gasped the landlord. "You're all over blood!"

"I am aware of that," retorted Lowe quietly. "I stumbled over the body in the dark."

"Oh, yer did, did yer?" There was open suspicion in the other's tone.

"Listen!" said Lowe sharply. "I didn't kill him and I know nothing about him. Now, go upstairs and waken my friends."

He waited, staring with half-closed eyes at the corpse. Presently he heard the thudding of knuckles on wood, followed by the sound of voices, and a moment or two later Shadgold appeared on the stairs, his eyes heavy with sleep and his bristling hair ruffled.

"What's the matter, Lowe?" he asked, and then, following the dramatist's eyes: "My God! What is it, an accident?"

"No," answered Lowe gravely. "Murder!"

"Murder!" The ominous word was echoed by Arnold White, Trevor Lowe's secretary, as he peered over the Scotland Yard man's shoulder.

Briefly and concisely Lowe explained.

"We must wake everybody in the house," said Shadgold, "and we ought to notify the local police." He turned to the sullen-faced landlord who was leaning against the doorpost. "Have you got a telephone here?"

Cornford shook his head.

"You say you heard the person, whoever it was, leave the room as you were coming downstairs?" Shadgold went on, rubbing vigorously at his toothbrush moustache.

"I heard somebody moving about," corrected Lowe. "Also there is the fact that the lamp had only recently been put out."

"You don't know anything about this, do you?" Shadgold glared at the landlord.

"What should I know about it?" retorted Cornford. "There ain't no reason why I should want to kill the feller. I never saw 'im till tonight!"

"What were you doing up?" asked Lowe, and noted the momentary hesitation before the landlord replied.

"I couldn't sleep," he answered, passing his tongue over his dry lips. "That blessed shutter was making such a row. I came down to see if I couldn't fix it!"

The sound of protesting voices reached them from upstairs, and in the light of the lamp that Shadgold had placed on a table Lowe saw a collection of scantily dressed figures being shepherded down the stairs by White.

"I've wakened everybody," said the secretary, "except the girl."

"I'm afraid you'll have to waken her," said Lowe. "We can't make any exceptions!"

"I can't waken her," said White. "She isn't there!"

*

"Take me up to the girl's room," muttered Lowe beneath his breath to his secretary.

White led the way upstairs to the end of a long passage and paused before an open door on the right.

"This is the room," he said, and Lowe entered the tiny chamber.

It was in pitch darkness, but this was dispelled when Lowe lighted the candle. On the floor was the girl's suitcase. It was open and the contents lay strewn in every direction. There was evidence of frantic haste here—haste on the part of somebody, presumably the girl herself. A dark object caught his eye among the crumpled bedclothes—a dark, furry object—and as he straightened out the none-too-clean coverlet, he saw that it was the threadbare coat with the fur collar which she had been wearing.

Moving away from the bed his foot struck something, and bending down to see what it was he found the girl's handbag. It was lying half under the bed, and, like the suitcase, had been opened and its contents scattered on the floor.

He collected the scattered contents and put them on the bed. There was a nearly used-up lipstick; a flat, metal container for face powder; a nail file; a little purse containing a shilling, some coppers, and a pound note; a handkerchief, and a letter—or rather the envelope of a letter—addressed to Iris Lake, 125b, Coram Street, W.C.2.

He noticed that the faded curtain which draped the window had been caught up, where someone in shutting the window had rammed a bit of the hem between the window and the wooden crosspiece. Only a person in a terrible hurry—or panic—would have overlooked that and left it.

He went over to the window and pushed it up as far as it would go. Outside, and barely two feet from the window, was the flat roof of a one-storey extension to the main building. Outlined in white by the snow, several chimney stacks were visible, but what interested him most was the unmistakable tracks of feet in the snow on the rooftop.

It did not take him long to visualize what had happened. Someone had entered the girl's room. Possibly she had been stunned. Then something had alarmed the intruder, he had picked up the senseless girl and carried her out on to the roof and hidden behind the stack until the alarm had passed. He shut the window.

They went downstairs again and found the coffee-room deserted. Shadgold had evidently marshalled the others in the bar.

"We'll take a look outside," said Lowe, and as he opened the front door a swirling cloud of snow blinded him.

He switched on the torch that he had taken from White's hand and swept the light over the white expanse of snow that seemed to stretch away to infinity in front of the door. The virgin whiteness was undisturbed by mark or footstep.

Fighting their way in the teeth of the howling gale, the driving snow making their cheeks smart and tingle, they made a complete circuit of the old building, and presently found themselves back in the porch from whence they had started. And in every direction all around the inn the thick carpet of snow lay smooth and undisturbed.

"That settles it," said Lowe, as he opened the door and they thankfully entered the comparative warmth of the hall. "No one came from outside and no one has left from within."

"Which means that the girl is somewhere on the premises," said Arnold White, vigorously rubbing his numbed hands.

"Also the murderer of William Makepiece!" added Trevor Lowe gravely.

*

Shadgold appeared at the half-glass door leading into the bar as they came in.

"Hallo!" he grunted. "Where have you been?"

Lowe explained, wiping the melting snow from his face and neck with his handkerchief.

"H'm!" grunted the Scotland Yard man. "Then the killer is amongst that bunch I've got in there."

"Have you succeeded in discovering anything?" asked the dramatist.

Shadgold shook his head gloomily.

"They all swear they were in bed and asleep and heard nothing until White roused them. And they all deny having known Makepiece or ever having seen him before until they met him on the train." He rubbed irritably at the back of his coarse neck. "Of course, somebody's lying," he grunted, "but the difficulty is to find out who. Not one of them has got an alibi, except Cornford."

"What's his alibi?" asked Lowe.

"His wife," answered the Scotland Yard man. "If you can call her an alibi. She confirms his story that he came down to see if he could fasten the banging shutter, and that he didn't move from her side until then. She remembers noting the time by the alarm clock they keep in their room, and it was half-past two when Cornford got up."

"Well, somebody wasn't in bed," said Lowe. "Before we go any further I think we ought to find Miss Lake."

"Who's Miss Lake?" demanded Shadgold, and then: "Oh, you mean the girl?"

"I feel sure she's in the building," said the dramatist, and he gave the inspector a brief account of his discoveries.

"It certainly sounds bad," agreed Shadgold. "I think you're right, we ought to find out what has become of her."

It was not until they searched the fourth room on the landing that they were rewarded for their diligence. The cupboard here refused to open when Lowe tried the handle.

"What is it?" grunted Shadgold.

"I can't get this cupboard open," said the dramatist. "It's locked. See if you can find anything to break it open with."

"This'll do," said Shadgold, handing him a short, rusty, iron poker.

Trevor Lowe took it, forced the point between the edge of the cupboard door and the jamb and pressed against it with all his strength. There was a cracking of splintering wood, and then with a loud snap that was like the report of a pistol the lock gave. As it did so the door swung open of its own accord, and something heavy that had been leaning against it fell out with a soft thud at their feet.

It was Iris Lake!

Her ankles and wrists had been tied with cord and a rough gag had been secured about her mouth. She was clad only in a thin suit of pyjamas and her hands and face were blue with cold. On her forehead was an ugly bruise and for a moment Lowe thought she was dead. He lifted the girl up, laid her on the bed, and untied the handkerchief that was tightly bound about her mouth.

She gave a little moan and stirred restlessly, but her eyes remained closed.

With his pocketknife Lowe slashed through the cords at wrists and ankles. Her hands were like blocks of ice, and he rubbed them vigorously to restore the circulation.

"See if you can get some brandy," he said sharply.

Presently Shadgold returned with a bottle and a glass, and followed by the agitated and indignant Mr Willings.

"'Ere, what's all this?" whined the little cockney. "What d'yer want me up here for?" and then, as his eyes lighted on the figure on the bed: "Struth! 'Ow did she get 'ere?"

"That's what we're waiting for you to tell us," said the dramatist harshly.

"Me?" Mr Willings' voice was even shriller than usual in his excitement. "Why ask me? 'Ow should I know?"

"This is your room, isn't it?" asked Lowe, pouring some brandy out into a glass.

"Yus, it's my room all right," answered the other, "but what's that got to do with it?"

"I'll tell you in a moment."

After great difficulty Lowe succeeded in getting the girl to swallow about a tablespoonful of brandy. When he had done this he set the glass down and turned his attention to the unhappy Mr Willings.

"Now," he said, "you say you don't know how this lady came to be in your room? You were either lying when you said you hadn't left your room previously, or you're responsible for the condition of this girl."

"'Ow do you make that out?"

There was a silence, and Mr Willings licked his dry lips.

"Oh, well," he said, "I suppose I'd better make a clean breast of it. As a matter of fact I wasn't in this 'ere room all the time. You see, it was like this 'ere. I went to bed and went to sleep, but the noise the wind was making and the banging and the creaking woke me up. Lyin' awake I began to feel thirsty, an' I thought 'ow good a nice drop of beer would taste, so I hopped up and pulled on me coat and went down to the bar. I was afraid it might be locked; but the door was open and I went in and drew meself a pint. That's the truth, and there ain't nothin' criminal in that!"

"What time was it when you went down for the beer?" said Lowe.

"I couldn't tell you that," answered the other. "But it wasn't very long before your friend came round waking everybody up."

"When you went down for the beer," said Lowe, "did you see or hear anybody about?"

The little man hesitated before replying.

"Well I did and I didn't," he said at length. "What I mean is, I thought there was somebody about, but I may 'ave been mistaken. The wind was making funny noises."

"You heard something," said Trevor Lowe quickly, and again there was a hesitation before he got a reply.

"Well, yus, I did," said Mr Willings reluctantly. "And it wasn't so much what I 'eard as what I felt. I could 'ave sworn that while I was drawin' that there beer I was bein' watched."

"Did you see someone then?" asked Lowe, as he paused.

The little man shook his head.

"No, I didn't see no one, and I didn't properly 'ear anyone. It was just a feelin'."

"H'm!" said Lowe. "Well, you ought to have told us all this before. After you'd had your beer and got back to your room did you hear anything then?"

"No, nothing," was the answer. "I was so perishin' cold that I pulled the bedclothes right up over me head and tried to get warm again."

Before Lowe could frame the next question a long quivering sigh from the girl attracted his attention, and, bending over the bed, he saw that her eyes were open. She was gazing up at him blankly without any sign of recognition, and as he stooped closer he saw that her lips were moving. No words came at first, and then faintly—so faintly as to be almost inaudible—she spoke.

"The Christmas card," she whispered. "Don't let them get it. Don't let—"

The feeble voice faded away into silence. Her eyes closed, and with another long sigh she relapsed into unconsciousness again.

There came a hurried step outside the door of the little parlour and a second later it was thrown open. Shadgold, breathing a little quickly and with his red face flushed with excitement, came in hastily.

"I've made a discovery, Lowe," he jerked. "I've found out what Makepiece was."

Lowe looked up interestedly. He had been sitting thoughtfully in front of the fire.

"What was he?" he asked.

"You heard of Cranston and Small?" said the inspector, and a curious light came into Trevor Lowe's eyes as he nodded.

"You mean the firm of private investigators who handle so much divorce work?" he said.

"They're the people," answered Shadgold. "Well, William Makepiece was on their staff. He was a detective!"

There was no doubt about the dead man's identity; the contents of a wallet which Shadgold had found in his room provided ample testimony in the shape of letters, and several visiting cards.

"A detective, was he?" said Lowe thoughtfully. "H'm. Well, that gives us a new angle. His firm will be able to state what business he was engaged on, and that may help."

"If he was engaged on any," answered the inspector. "You've always got to take into consideration, Mr Lowe, that this is the holiday season. He may only have been on his way to spend Christmas somewhere."

"The thing that puzzles me, Shadgold, is the torn half of that Christmas card. Where is the other half? Did the person who killed

Makepiece remove it, and if so why didn't he remove the whole? There was obviously no struggle, so it didn't get torn accidentally. And what has the girl got to do with it?"

There came a tap on the door and without waiting for an invitation the surly faced landlord slouched in, a worried look on his unpleasant face. He stopped just within the open doorway and looked from one to the other hesitantly.

"What is it? What do you want?" growled Shadgold.

Cornford advanced another step and cleared his throat. When he spoke his voice was dry and husky.

"I wanted to have a word with yer," he said.

"Do you know something?" snapped the Scotland Yard man eagerly.

The landlord nodded slowly.

"Yus, I know somethin'," he replied. "'Tain't much, but I think I oughta tell yer." He seemed to find some difficulty in putting his story into words, and they waited expectantly and impatiently. "It's like this," said Cornford, after a pause, "one of those fellers 'as been lying to yer. I can prove—"

What he could prove they never knew, for at that instant from outside the room came a sharp, spitting crack, and the landlord's face sagged. His jaw dropped and his little black eyes opened wide. A stupid look of astonishment crossed his ugly face, and both his hands went to his back. He tried to speak, groaned, and fell forward.

With a startled exclamation Lowe caught him as he slumped to the ground, easing his fall.

A second shot whistled past Shadgold's ear as he made a dash for the door, and then a heavy object struck him in the face, and with a cry of pain he staggered backwards. There was a sharp thud as something fell on the floor of the little room.

The man in Lowe's arms gave a convulsive shudder and his head fell limply backwards. Lowe took one look at the landlord's face and knew that Joe Cornford would never utter the words he had been about to speak. He was dead! And the weapon that had killed him lay a few feet away, shining dully blue in the light from the lamp on the table.

As he lowered the limp form of the landlord to the floor Trevor Lowe heard an excited shout followed by the sound of running feet, and a second later Arnold White appeared in the open doorway.

"What was the shooting?" he began, and stopped abruptly as he saw the thing at the dramatist's feet.

"That's what the shooting was," said Lowe grimly, pointing down at all that was left of Joe Cornford. "He was shot through the doorway. Did you see anyone?"

White shook his head.

"Not a soul," he replied. "I was upstairs having a wash when I heard the shots, and hurried down at once, but I saw no one."

Shadgold, dabbing at the red weal across his face, grunted savagely.

"I'm going to find out where everyone was," he growled, and without waiting for a reply strode across the hall to the coffee-room. Jerking open the door he glared in.

The meek-faced Mr Pilbeam was sitting hunched up in a chair before the fire. He was apparently asleep, for he jumped up with a start when Shadgold spoke.

"Where are the others?" demanded the Scotland Yard man, glaring round the empty room.

"I—I don't know," stammered Mr Pilbeam. "They were here when I fell asleep."

The burly inspector eyed him suspiciously.

"Been asleep, have you?" he snapped. "You sure of that?"

"C-c-course I'm sure," stammered the meek little man. "Y-y-you woke me up, bursting in like that."

"H'm! Well, you stay where you are." The inspector swung round as a murmur of startled voices reached his ears. The rest of the party were crowding down the staircase, and bringing up the rear was the unkempt figure of Mrs Cornford, the landlady.

"What was all that bangin'?" demanded Arty Willings, as he saw Shadgold. "Sounded like somebody shootin'."

"It was somebody shooting," answered the Scotland Yard man curtly. "Where have you people been?"

A chorus of voices answered him. It seemed useless to expect to get any more sleep that night and, scantily clad as they were, they had begun to feel chilly in spite of the fire in the coffee-room, so they had decided to slip up to their rooms and dress.

"Well, you can all go into the coffee-room," snapped Shadgold, "and you can stay there, do you understand? No one is to leave that room without my permission."

At that moment the voice of the landlady came to him, and Lowe went out into the hall to see what she wanted. He found her standing on the stairs.

"You asked me to tell yer," said the woman, "when that girl was awake. Well, she is."

"Good!" said the dramatist. "I'll come up at once."

The woman led the way to the room and stood aside for him to enter.

The girl's big grey eyes were open, and looked large and almost black in the dead whiteness of her face. Trevor Lowe went over to the bed and sat on the edge.

"Feeling better, Miss Lake?" he asked kindly.

She nodded slowly.

"Yes, thank you," she answered. "What—what happened?"

Lowe told her how they had found her. She gave a little shiver.

"I don't remember anything," she said. "I went to bed and fell asleep almost at once. Soon afterwards I was dimly conscious of someone standing over me, and then something very painful struck me on the head. After that I remembered nothing until I woke up and found myself here."

"Have you any idea, Miss Lake, why this attack should have been made on you?"

She hesitated, her big eyes searching his face, and then she nodded again.

"Yes, I think I do," she answered faintly. "I'm sure I do."

Trevor Lowe leaned forward.

"Then will you tell me, Miss Lake?" he said. "I assure you it's not with any wish to pry into your affairs that I ask, but a serious crime was committed here last night, apart from the attack on you, and another one has just taken place."

"Crime?" she said, and her eyes grew dark with fear.

"Yes, murder," he replied gravely.

She drew in her breath with a quick little hiss.

"Who—who was killed?" she asked.

"That stout, jolly faced man," said Lowe, watching her keenly. "William Makepiece."

The name apparently conveyed nothing to her, for the expression on her face did not change.

"How—how dreadful!" she whispered. And then: "Who are you?"

"My name is Trevor Lowe," answered the dramatist.

The fear died from her eyes and a look of relief came into her pale face.

"I've heard of you," she said.

"Who were you frightened of?" he asked. And she shook her head.

"I don't know," she replied. "That's the dreadful part of it!"

"I think you had better tell me everything," he said, as she paused.

"I will," she answered. "But it's rather a difficult story—I mean, it's not very easy to tell to a stranger—and I don't quite know where to begin."

"Tell me why you were attacked," said Lowe. "Do you know why?"

"Oh yes," she answered at once. "I was attacked because of something I possess!" She smiled rather sadly, and added hastily: "I haven't any money. I've so little that I don't know how I've managed to live during the last year, but I've got something that's worth roughly, about half a million pounds!"

Lowe stared at her in amazement.

"You've got something that's worth half a million pounds?" he echoed incredulously. "Do you mean you've got it here?"

She nodded, and a little glimmer of amusement crept into her eyes at the astonishment that her words had created.

"Yes, I've got it here," she said. "At least, I've got half of it. What I have isn't worth a cent all by itself. You see, this is the way of it, Mr Lowe. I'm going to start really from the beginning, I'll make it as brief as I can." Her voice was stronger now and a tinge of colour had crept into the creamy whiteness of her cheeks. "I'd better start by telling you," she went on, "that my name isn't Lake. Lake is the name I've been known by all my life, but my real name is Lanning."

Trevor Lowe started.

"You're not any relation to Sir Joshua Lanning?" he asked.

"Yes," she said. "I'm his daughter!"

Lowe's brows contracted. The daughter of Sir Joshua Lanning, the steel millionaire!

"Please go on, Miss Lanning," he said. "I'm very interested!"

"As I said," she continued, "it's very difficult. Although I'm Sir Joshua Lanning's daughter I've never seen him. You see, my mother divorced him when I was two years old, and she was given the custody of the child. She was very bitter against my father, and she took me away, returning to her maiden name of Lake. My father, I believe, begged and prayed her not to go, but when she insisted gave her an envelope, and said that if at any time she wished to return to him and remarry him she had only to send the contents of the envelope and he would come to her, wherever she was.

"My mother told me this just before she died, seven years ago, but she also made me promise that I would never go near my father unless he should first seek me out. I had no money and I had to earn my living, which I succeeded in doing more or less—mostly less. And then a week ago I saw in a newspaper an advertisement. It had been put in by a firm of solicitors and briefly stated that if Miss Iris Lake, or Lanning, would call on the advertisers she would hear something to her advantage.

"I guessed that it concerned my father, and I went. Mr Thompson, the head of the firm, told me at once that they had had over a hundred applicants, but that he had soon assured himself that they were none of them the person he was looking for. If I were really that person there would be one means of identification, and only one, which would satisfy him.

"I knew what he meant, of course, the envelope which my father had given my mother. I told the solicitor that I knew what he meant, without exactly telling him what the thing was. He told me that my father was dying and that he was very anxious to find his missing daughter. He had already made a will in her favour.

"He asked me if I would travel down to Tregoney, where my father was living, taking with me the means of identification which I had mentioned. He wrote to my father saying that I would arrive on the twenty-third, and I was on my way when the snow block forced us to spend the night here."

"And this means of identification that you were taking with you?" asked Lowe, although he knew before she answered.

"Was the half of a Christmas card," she replied, "a Christmas card that my mother had sent to my father the Christmas before they were married. He had torn it in half, keeping one half and putting the other half in the envelope which he gave her."

"I see," said Lowe softly. "And where is your half?"

"Go along to the room I occupied and fetch my shoes," she said.

When he came back with them she struggled up to a sitting posture and, taking the left one pulled out the lining of the sole. Between it and the sole itself was an envelope, and, opening this, she drew out the torn half of an old and faded Christmas card.

"That's it," she said.

Lowe looked at it.

"If that's your half," he said slowly, "and the other half is in the possession of your father, then how does the third 'half' come into it?"

She looked at him puzzled.

"The third half? What do you mean?" she asked.

"I mean," replied Trevor Lowe, "that I found half a Christmas card in the hand of the dead man, William Makepiece."

*

"Well, it's a queer story," remarked Detective Inspector Shadgold thoughtfully an hour later, when Trevor Lowe had repeated to him what he had learned from Iris Lanning. "And it's a queer business. I don't quite see how this fellow Makepiece fits in."

"I should imagine that the solicitors had engaged him, unknown to the girl, to keep an eye on her," said Lowe.

"You mean they expected something might happen?" said the Scotland Yard man.

"It's not unnatural, is it?" asked Lowe. "The torn piece of cardboard she was carrying about with her is worth something in the nature of half a million—a big enough bait for any crook to have a bite at!"

"Still, it wouldn't be any good without the girl," argued Shadgold.

"Oh, my dear fellow," protested Lowe, "think for a moment! The last time Sir Joshua Lanning saw his daughter she was two years old; he hasn't seen her since. Any girl would do provided she could produce the necessary form of identification."

"H'm, yes, I suppose you're right," grunted the Scotland Yard man. "But the solicitors had seen her."

"The solicitors had seen a girl who said she was the girl they were advertising for," answered the dramatist. "They had no proof that she was, except her word that she had the necessary identification. Until she had shown her half of the Christmas card to Sir Joshua Lanning nobody could tell whether she was the right girl or not."

"Then it's your opinion," said Shadgold, "that the idea was to secure the girl's half and substitute someone else in her place?"

"Exactly," replied Lowe, nodding. "Makepiece had to die because he knew the real Iris Lanning, but if we had found in the morning that the two of them were missing, everyone would have thought that they had gone of their own free will. No doubt the killer would have tidied up the rooms and made it look like that."

"That's suggesting that he knew who Makepiece was and why he was here," said Shadgold.

"I'm suggesting just that," answered Lowe.

"And how do you account for the torn half of the Christmas card found in Makepiece's hand?" demanded the Scotland Yard man.

Trevor Lowe frowned and shook his head.

"I can't account for it," he replied frankly, "but there must be some explanation. Let me look at it again."

Shadgold thrust his hand into his pocket and produced his wallet. From it he extracted the torn Christmas card and handed it to the dramatist.

Trevor Lowe carried it over to the lamp and examined it carefully. It was obviously a new card; the ragged edges were clean and unsoiled. In turning it sideways he noticed something that he had not seen before. In one corner were a number of indentations. A closer inspection revealed the letter D and the figures 2 and 1. Above and below these were indistinguishable marks forming two semicircles.

An idea suddenly occurred to Lowe, and taking out the envelope he had found in the girl's room, and which he had put in his pocket, he compared the postmark with the marks on the card. It had been posted on December the twenty-first. The stamp had been rather heavily impressed and had marked the enclosed card. He showed his discovery to Shadgold.

"There's very little doubt," he said, "that this card I found in Makepiece's hand originally came out of this envelope. I wonder if it was the girl who tore this card," he continued slowly, "and left half in the envelope as a blind to make anyone think it was the important card—the piece that was hidden in her shoe."

"It sounds possible," said Shadgold. "Why not ask her?"

"I will," said Lowe, "and test this half Makepiece had with the genuine half."

He returned in less than a minute.

"That's cleared that up," he said. "She tore a Christmas card she had received in half and left one half in the envelope so that anyone finding it would think it was the real card. You know what conclusion this leads to? That it was Makepiece who searched the girl's room. In which case he was responsible for knocking her out, tying her up and putting her in that cupboard. But he wasn't responsible for sticking that knife into his heart. I think the person who did that did the rest."

"The question is, who?" growled the inspector. He took a glass round behind the bar, and, grasping one of the handles, held it under the tap. Nothing happened. With a snort of disgust he tried the other. He tried all three with a like result. "I suppose there's nothing more to do until the local police arrive?"

"No, I suppose not," said the dramatist, a little absently, and then: "What happened to Mrs Cornford?"

Shadgold looked at him rather surprised.

"I packed her off to her room," he answered. "She wasn't in a fit state to remain up."

"I'd like to have a word with her," murmured Lowe. "Wait here, I shan't be long."

He left the bar and made his way upstairs. Outside the room in which the girl lay he came upon his secretary who had been delegated to the job of keeping guard.

"Anybody been near?" he asked, and White shook his head.

"No," he replied.

Trevor Lowe nodded and passed on. Mrs Cornford's room was on the first floor above, and reaching it he tapped on the door. At first there was no reply, but at the second knock the old woman's voice called and wanted to know who was there.

"It's Trevor Lowe," replied the dramatist. "Can I have a word with you?"

He heard the creak of a bed, the pad of bare feet crossing the floor, and then the door was opened an inch.

"What do you want with me?" asked the woman dully.

"I want to ask you a question," he replied.

She looked at him curiously when she heard what he wanted to know.

"Not for nearly a year," she said.

"You're sure of that," he asked, and she nodded.

Shadgold was staring out of the window at the cold grey of the coming morning when Lowe came back.

"Well?" he grunted.

"Very well," answered Lowe cheerfully, and there was a note of satisfaction in his voice. "I think we're nearing the end of this business."

The Scotland Yard man stared at him incredulously.

"If you'll ask Willings to come in for a moment I'll show you."

Shadgold hesitated, and then shrugged his shoulders.

"Oh, well, I suppose you know what you're getting at," he said, and crossing over to the door went out."

He was gone some little time, and when he returned was accompanied by the sleepy-eyed Arty Willings, who yawned openly as he slouched in.

"I want your help, Mr Willings," said the dramatist genially.

The little cockney eyed him suspiciously.

"You said," explained Lowe, "that when you came down in the night you had a feeling that you were being watched."

"That's right," said Mr Willings, nodding.

"Now, where did you experience this feeling?" Lowe went on. "While you were coming down the stairs? While you were in here? Or as you were returning to your room?"

"While I was in here," answered the other, after a momentary hesitation.

"But you neither heard anything nor saw anyone?" said Lowe, and Mr Willings shook his head.

"No, I told you that before," he replied. "It was only a feelin' I 'ad."

"Was the coffee-room door closed?"

"Yes," answered Mr Willings after a little thought.

"I see," murmured the dramatist. "Now, would you mind showing us exactly what you did when you came down?"

"I came in 'ere," said the little cockney, "went over to the bar, and had a glass of beer."

"Show us what you did," repeated Lowe, and Mr Willings obeyed.

He went round behind the long counter, picked up a glass, and stretched out his hand to the centre of the three beer handles.

"Just a minute," interrupted Lowe. "You poured yourself out a glass of draught beer? You didn't open a bottle or draw it from the cask?"

"No," said Arty Willings. "I prefer draught beer. And mighty good it was!"

"And then you returned to your room and went to bed?" said the dramatist.

"That's right," answered Mr Willings.

"H'm!" said Lowe. "And during this time the murderer was secreting Miss Lake in the cupboard in your room. Let's see if we can imagine what he did. He left his room when he thought the whole house was quiet and sleeping and made his way along to the girl's. He knew that she had in her possession an object that was worth a considerable amount of money. He rendered her unconscious with a blow from some instrument like a sandbag. He was disturbed for a moment, and dodged out on the roof with the senseless girl. Afterwards he climbed back and carried the girl, whom he had bound and gagged, along to your room and locked her in the cupboard.

"He then went back to search her belongings for the thing he wanted, and he found it—or thought he had found it—in her handbag. He was afraid to stop in her room and examine it closely, for there was no means of locking the door, and there was a chance that he might be surprised by one of the other inhabitants of the inn. He brought it down to the coffee-room, lighted the lamp and found to his dismay that he had been tricked. The thing he had taken so much trouble to get was a fake.

"He had just decided to make another search of the girl's room when William Makepiece appeared in the doorway, and demanded that he hand over the object he had taken and which was still in his hand.

"Makepiece informed him that he was a detective who had been employed to see that no harm came to the girl. The man, whom we will call X for the moment, saw his whole plan being ruined by this unexpected intruder. No doubt Makepiece threatened him; probably there was a brief struggle for possession of the precious object that X had taken such pains to secure. The safest way to stop Makepiece from keeping it, and also from babbling afterwards, was to kill him. This X did and so became a murderer.

"He placed the worthless article in Makepiece's hand, to leave a false clue to suggest that it was Makepiece who had ransacked the girl's case.

"He was clever," continued Lowe, "but like so many crooks, he wasn't clever enough. He made a mistake. If you fetch me the thing he took from the girl's room I'll show you what that mistake was, Willings."

Lowe nodded casually towards the far corner of the bar on which lay several objects, and among them the torn card, which he had taken from Makepiece's hand. Mr Willings went over, picked it up, and handed it to the detective.

"Thank you," said Lowe, and his eyes gleamed. "I said just now that the murderer made a mistake. As a matter of fact he made two. He's just made the second—a mistake I was hoping he would make. I never mentioned what the object was that he took from Miss Lake's room. Nobody knew, except Inspector Shadgold, my secretary, and myself, that the torn half of a Christmas card was found in the dead man's hand. How did you know, Willings?"

The colour fled from the little cockney's face, leaving it a dirty white.

"I don't know," he began. "I—"

"You knew!" snapped Lowe sternly, "because it was you who took this card out of Miss Lake's handbag in the first place. You who tied her up and locked her in your cupboard. You who came downstairs and later killed William Makepiece. You who, when the girl was found, lied and said that you had felt thirsty and came down to this bar and drawn yourself beer."

"You're talking nonsense!" cried the man. "You're trying to frame this on me! I did come down to get a drink! All I've told you is true!" In his excitement all trace of his cockney accent had vanished, and Lowe was quick to remark on it.

"You've forgotten your accent, Mr Willings," he said softly. "The same as you forgot to verify your facts concerning your story of the beer."

"What do you mean?" muttered the other.

"I mean," retorted Trevor Lowe curtly, "that that beer engine has not been connected for a year! That's what Cornford was going to tell us when you shot him. It was absolutely impossible for you to have drawn any beer that way. That, coupled with the fact that you fell into the trap I had prepared for you has given you away. No one but the man who searched Miss Lake's room could have known what the object was I referred to, and yet you went and fetched it without my telling you—fetched it from among half a dozen other objects, all of which might equally have been the right one."

The trapped man's lips drew back from his teeth in a snarl. Without warning he picked up a wooden stool that stood in front of the bar and hurled it at Trevor Lowe's head.

"I suppose you think you've got me?" he cried harshly. "But you haven't, yet!"

Lowe dodged the stool and it went crashing through the window, ripping out glass and woodwork—and then Shadgold took a hand. As Willings made a dash for the door he barred his path and gripped him by the arm.

"No you don't!" he growled; and the revolver with which the other had shot the landlord appeared in his other hand. "You just keep quiet. If you can find any rope, Lowe, we'll tie him up until the police arrive."

⋆

The police patrol was stopped as he passed the inn and given the news and instructions. Later came a sleepy-eyed inspector and a constable. They came in a car, and when they went away were accompanied by the man who called himself Arty Willings.

Later on that morning, when the snow had stopped falling and a pale sun shone coldly on the expanse of white, a car, which Lowe had asked the police to send from Bugle, arrived and drove the dramatist, Shadgold, Arnold White and the girl to Tregoney, where they left her to meet the father she had never seen.

It was on the morning of Christmas Day that Trevor Lowe heard the last echo of that sinister business at the gloomy inn. Shadgold had just returned from Bugle and an interview with the police. Arty Willings had been identified as Montague Buxton, a cousin of Sir Joshua Lanning, and when he found that the game was up he made a full confession. It tallied almost exactly with Lowe's theory.

The old man had told Buxton the story of his efforts to find his missing daughter, and gradually the idea had taken shape in Buxton's brain to put forward a substitute. He had led a fairly wild life and was associated with a woman who had few scruples that money could not overrule. He had confided his plans to her, and she had agreed to present herself to Sir Joshua as his missing relative. Buxton, who had been staying with the old man, was aware that he was prepared to accept anyone who could produce the torn half of the Christmas card which matched his own.

In order to keep an eye on the girl he had disguised himself as the rather insignificant looking cockney, and had met the Western Express from Paddington at Bodmin. He had tried to kidnap the girl when the train came to a halt after snow blocked the line but he'd been surprised by Trevor Lowe and Arnold White. When they had all been forced to spend the night at the Chained Man, he was forced to come up with a new plan.

"There's plenty of evidence against him," the Scotland Yard man concluded. "I should think the jury would bring in a verdict without leaving the box."

"Well, he deserves what he gets," said Trevor Lowe, "if ever a man did."

THE MOTIVE

Ronald Knox

Ronald Knox (1888–1957) was a brilliant member of an outrageously gifted family of over-achievers. One of his brothers, "Evoe", became editor of *Punch*; another, "Dilly", was a legendary code-breaker whose war-time exploits are now honoured at Bletchley Park. His sister Winifred enjoyed success under her married name, Winifred Peck, with a string of popular novels; her output included a couple of detective stories which have recently been republished. Educated at Eton and Balliol, Ronnie Knox was an intellectual, a classicist and Oxford University tutor whose pupils included the future Prime Minister, Harold Macmillan. After leaving the Anglican church, he became well known as a Catholic priest and as a broadcaster on BBC radio.

Knox's passion for the Sherlock Holmes stories led him to become a pioneer of Sherlockian criticism. This fondness for detective fiction led him to try his hand at writing it himself, and his first mystery novel, *The Viaduct Murder*, appeared in 1925. This stand-alone story was followed at regular intervals by five more detective novels, each featuring the amiable insurance investigator Miles Bredon, and he became a prominent Golden Age detective author, focused mainly on puzzles rather than in-depth characterization. Knox devised the famous "Ten Commandments" of detective fiction, facetious "rules" which some people took far too seriously. Elements from this "Decalogue" were embodied in the initiation ritual to be undergone by new recruits to the Detection Club, of which Knox was a founder member; the ritual continues, in much-changed form, to this day. From the outset, however, Club members delighted in flouting the so-called "rules". Knox only wrote a handful of short crime stories, but their quality makes this a matter for regret. This elaborate story with a cheeky if not shameless final twist first appeared in *The Illustrated London News* on 17 November 1937. For one of the characters, Westmacott, Knox borrowed a pen-name used by his Detection Club colleague Agatha Christie; it was a custom of Club members at the time, and something of an in-joke, to give each other such hat-tips in their fiction.

"A CERTAIN AMOUNT OF DUST IS GOOD FOR A JURYMAN'S eyes. It prevents him going to sleep."

Sir Leonard Huntercombe is probably responsible for more scoundrels being at large than any other man in England. His references to the feelings of his client, to the long ordeal which a criminal prosecution involves, to the fallibility of witnesses, to those British liberties which we all enjoy only on the condition that everybody must be given the benefit of the doubt unless he is found with his hand in the till, are a subject of legitimate tedium and irreverent amusement to the reporters, who have heard it all before. But it still goes down with the jury, fresh to their job; and, after all, that is more important. It does not often happen to such a man that he is drawn into the old, old argument, whether a defending counsel is justified in pressing his defence when he privately knows his client to be guilty. And, of all places, you might have expected him to be free from such annoyances in the Senior Common Room of Simon Magus—the smoking-room, to be more accurate. Dons hate a scene, and prefer to talk trivialities after dinner. It is hardly even good form, nowadays, to talk a man's own shop to him. In these days of specialization we are all bored with each other's technicalities, and a tacit convention has grown up that we should stick to the weather and the Boat Race. Sir Leonard was justified, then, if his eye resembled that of a codfish rather more than usual.

For, as bad luck would have it, Penkridge was dining as some-body else's guest—Penkridge, the dramatic critic, to whom all the world is a stage, and everything, consequently, a fit subject for dramatic criticism. It takes less than the Simon Magus port (though that is a powerful affair) to make such a man as Penkridge boor-ishly argumentative. He had trailed his coat deliberately, with a forthcoming article in view, and had contrived to put Sir Leonard on his own defence almost before he knew it. I need hardly say that he was adopting the most Puritan view.

McBride, the philosopher, was the host of the great man; and he felt bound to interfere, partly from a sense of hospitality, and partly because he always likes to be desperately just. (Nobody, it has been said, has seen more points of view than McBride, or adopted less.) "I was just thinking," he said, "that perhaps you could put up an apology for Sir Leonard's point of view if you claim that Law should be regarded as one of the sciences. You see, it's notorious, isn't it—I think even Cowan here will agree with me—that science owes some of its greatest developments to the influence of theories which have proved quite false, but were suggestive nevertheless, and put people on the track of the truth. Isn't it arguable, I mean, in the same way, that my friend here is justified in putting forward a hypothesis, which will help forward the cause of truth if only by eliminating error?"

Penkridge, who hates dons, was evidently preparing to say something unpleasant; but Sir Leonard forestalled him by disown-ing the proffered help. "It's not a scientific mind you need in the legal profession," he insisted; "it's a kind of artistic gift. You've got to be imaginative; to throw yourself into the business of picturing the story happening as you want it to have happened; with your client innocent, of course. Probably, if we knew, we should find that the truth in many cases is even stranger than all our imaginings. But imagination is what you must have—did I ever tell you the story of a client of mine, a man by the name of Westmacott?"

Several voices demanded that the story should be told; better to have Sir Leonard being prosy, than Penkridge being unmannerly. And Sir Leonard, when his cigar was going, went ahead with the story.

"I first came across Westmacott," explained Sir Leonard, "over a business that never came into court, though it precious nearly did. I was only called in on a minor point to give counsel's opinion. He was a man in late middle age, with an unhealthy look about him, as if you wouldn't give him a very long life, and a depressed, restless sort of manner, as if his mind was preoccupied with something else than what he was talking about at the moment. He had done well on the Stock Exchange, and had retired just lately, with a considerable income he hardly knew what to do with. At least, it was a surprise to his friends when he went to stay over Christmas at one of those filthy great luxury hotels in Cornwall. It was the kind of place that tried to make you believe you were on the Riviera, with any amount of central heating and artificial sunlight, and a covered-in bathing-pool where the water was kept at a temperature of eighty or so, night and day. Of course, he might have gone to Cornwall for his health; but one didn't see why he should have gone to a place like that, because he was well known to be old-fashioned in his views and conservative in his opinions, whereas the Hotel Resplendent was all full of modern people, a cosmopolitan and rather Bohemian crowd. Among the rest there was a well-known literary man; he's still alive, and you'd all know his name, so I'll call him just Smith.

"I'm speaking of some years ago, you'll understand. Nowadays, of course, it doesn't matter what anybody writes, or what sort of opinions he puts forward; it's all art. But at the time of which I'm speaking, there were still people going about who were capable of being shocked, and they were shocked by Smith. It wasn't so much his indecency, though every book he wrote looked as if it was meant to be seized by the police. He was really, if an old fogy like myself can be allowed to use such forgotten language, a bad influence on the young people; everybody admitted it, though already most people rather admired him for it. Westmacott had never met him before, and the other people in the hotel felt pretty certain that the two wouldn't hit it off. The curious thing is, they were wrong. Westmacott hadn't read any of Smith's stuff, it appeared; indeed, he read very little except detective stories, which he devoured at the rate of one a day. And—well, strange acquaintances do ripen, and ripen fast, in a god-forsaken place like the Hotel Resplendent.

"It was a bad season; money wasn't being thrown about that year as much as usual; and the management tried to make the best of the position by encouraging the guests to be a sort of family party, with any amount of 'olde-worlde' festivities. Naturally, they concentrated on Christmas Day; crackers and Christmas presents, and a synthetic boar's head, and a Yule-log specially imported from Sweden; and a set of waits who'd been in training under an opera expert for months past. By half-past ten the company—between twenty and thirty of them, when you'd counted out the invalids who'd gone to bed early, and the idiots who'd gone out in cars for no reason whatever—found themselves set down by the master of the revels to play 'blind man's buff.' This didn't go too well, especially as the great hall in which they played it was heated like a crematorium. It was Westmacott, people remembered afterwards, who made the suggestion you would have expected to come from anybody but Westmacott—that they should all go and play 'blind man's buff' in the swimming-bath.

"Well, they got some kick out of it after that. Westmacott didn't go in himself, but he hung about on the edge; as a matter of fact, it was only pretty strong swimmers who did go in, because the bath was a matter of twelve feet deep at the shallowest part, and there was nothing but a hand-rail to lug yourself out by. Smith and Westmacott got into an argument, Westmacott saying he didn't believe you could know what direction you were swimming in when you were blindfolded, and Smith (who was an exceptionally good swimmer himself) maintaining that it was perfectly easy, unless you'd got a bad sense of direction anyhow. It was nearly midnight when the party went away, and it seems that Smith and Westmacott stayed behind to settle their differences with a practical try-out and a bet; Smith was to swim ten lengths in the bath each way, touching the ends every time, but never touching the sides. They were quite alone when Westmacott adjusted the handker-chief on his new friend's forehead, to make sure that everything was above-board.

"Well, Smith did his ten lengths each way, and by his own account made a good thing of it. As he swam he didn't bother to touch the hand-rail, which was rather high out of the water; but when he'd finished he naturally felt for it—*and it wasn't there!* He tore the handkerchief off his eyes, which wasn't too easy, and found the whole place was in the dark. The rail wasn't within his reach anywhere, and he tumbled to what must have happened. Somehow a goodish lot of water must have been let out of the bath while he wasn't looking; and there was nothing to do but go on swimming about until somebody came to put things right for him; or, alternatively, until the level of the water fell so much that he was able to stand on the bottom.

"Other things began to occur to him before long. For one thing, he knew, more or less, where it was that the water escaped when the bath was changed, and he knew that there was a considerable undertow when it happened. He found there was no undertow now, which meant that the water wasn't escaping any longer, and there was no chance of finding that he'd got into his depth. Also, he remembered that the swimming-bath was a long way from anywhere, and it wasn't very likely that he would be heard if he shouted. Also, he couldn't quite see how the water could have started emptying itself and then stopped, unless somebody was controlling it.

"Well, they say the devil looks after his own, and it so happened that the night watchman, whom they kept at the Hotel Resplendent (chiefly to keep out of the way when he wasn't wanted), had spotted that the water was running away, and mentioned it to somebody; a search was made, and Smith was pulled out of the water with a rope, none too soon for his peace of mind. Smith was positive, of course, that he had been the victim of a particularly cunning murderous attack. I say particularly cunning, because, once he had drowned, it would have been easy for Westmacott (he assumed Westmacott was the villain) to have let the water into the bath again; and all the world would have been left supposing that Smith had committed suicide—how else could a strong swimmer have drowned with a hand-rail in his reach all the time? It looked as if it was going to be a very nasty business, and what didn't make it any better was Westmacott's own explanation, made privately to his lawyers, that the whole thing was a joke, and he had been meaning to rescue Smith later on. Nothing, it was explained to him, is more difficult to predict than a jury's sense of humour. Enormous efforts were made to hush the thing up, chiefly by the hotel people, who thought it meant the end of their business if they were involved in a scandal; I'm not sure they were right there, but, as I say, this happened some years ago. The difficulty of Smith's case was that there was no proving it was Westmacott who had tampered with the water apparatus (as a matter of fact, anybody could have done it), and it was that hitch that induced the police to let it go; and Smith to be content with a handsome compensation.

"Well, it was touch and go, and there was nothing I expected less than to find Westmacott, to all appearances a dull and unadventurous man, figuring in my line of business again. Though, as a matter of fact, the police had found out things about him which would have altered my opinion if I'd known about them. His man, fortunately for the police, had done time at an earlier stage in his career, and was all too ready to give them information. He assured them that a great change had come over his master within the last week or so before he went to the Resplendent; he had come home one morning looking like a man bowed down by some hideous secret anxiety, though up to then he had been in normally good spirits. He cursed the servants freely, he would start at shadows. He bought a revolver, which the police found in his rooms (he was a bachelor, I forgot to say); and although this only looked like self-defence, it was a more peculiar circumstance that, about the same time, he got hold of a drug (I forget the name of it now) which is deadly poison, and I'm not sure that he hadn't forged a doctor's certificate to get it.

"It was less than a week after the trouble had died down that a new character came on the scene: a character nobody liked, who had seen him. He was a seedy-looking fellow calling himself

Robinson, who seemed very anxious to have an interview with Westmacott, for he made a great fuss with the servants when he called three times and found he was always out. It was the opinion of the servants that Robinson went about in disguise for no good end, but servants will always say that of anybody who wears dark spectacles. When the two did first meet, the servants weren't prepared to say, because Westmacott lived on one floor, and often let in his visitors himself. Anyhow, for a fortnight or so he was a familiar figure in the house, being seen several times coming in and out.

"Westmacott had the habit of going to stay with friends near Aberdeen about the New Year. This time, he went a little later than usual; and it was a considerable surprise to his man when he was given the order to reserve two first-class sleepers on the night train from King's Cross, one in the name of Westmacott, and another in the name of Robinson. It didn't look too good; you couldn't by any stretch of the imagination suppose that Robinson belonged to the same world as Westmacott and his friends. In fact, if he hadn't been professionally shy of them, I think the man would have gone to the police about it; it looked so much as if Robinson had got a hold of some kind over Westmacott, and was following him about for fear of losing his tracks. Anyhow, nothing was done about it. Westmacott was a man who fussed about trains, and he was at the station, it seems, a full three-quarters of an hour before the train started; he was worried, apparently, about Robinson—asked the attendant once or twice whether he had shown up yet, and stood looking up and down the platform. As he did this, a telegram was brought to him which seemed to set his mind at rest; he shut himself up in his sleeper, and took no further notice, as far as could be ascertained. Robinson turned up with only two or three minutes to spare, and was bundled hurriedly into the sleeper next door.

Whether the two held any conversation was not known; the two sleepers communicated with one another in the ordinary way, and it was only a matter of slipping a bolt for either to enter the other's compartment.

"Robinson, it appeared, was not travelling all the way to Aberdeen; he was to get off at Dundee. The man was to come and call him about three-quarters of an hour before the train got in there. As a matter of fact, he cannot have slept too well, or possibly the lights and the shouting at Edinburgh woke him; at any rate, he went along the corridor just about when they were passing Dalmeny, and spoke to the attendant, who asked whether the order to call him still stood. He said yes, he expected to drop off again for a bit, and he was a heavy sleeper. Indeed, when the attendant knocked at his door, there seemed to be no waking him, and it was locked. With many apologies, the man knocked up Westmacott, and asked his leave to try the communicating door between the two compartments. This, it proved, was locked on Westmacott's side, but not on Robinson's. The attendant went in, and found the carriage quite empty. The bed had been slept in; that is, somebody had lain down on it, there was no mistaking the fact. Robinson's luggage was still there; his watch was hanging by the bunk; a novel he had been reading lay on the floor close by; his boots were there, and his day clothes, not his pajamas.

"Well, there was all sorts of fuss and bother, as you can imagine. Westmacott, who seemed quite dazed by the news and unable to give any account of it, naturally got out at Dundee and put himself at the disposal of the police authorities. They did not like the look of the thing from the start. They had rung up Scotland Yard, and through some unwonted piece of efficiency had got on to the story of Smith and his experiences in the bath at the Resplendent.

Exhaustive inquiries brought no news of Robinson being seen anywhere on the line; and there had been no stop, no slow-down, even, between the time when the attendant saw him in the corridor and the time when his bed was found empty. The train, naturally, had been searched, but without result."

"But they must have found his body," someone suggested.

"No remains were found; but you have to consider the lie of the journey. Between Dalmeny and Thornton junction, near which the attendant tried to wake Robinson, the train has to pass over the Forth Bridge. The one interval of time, therefore, during which it was impossible to account for Robinson's movements was an interval of time during which a body might, conceivably, have been got rid of without leaving any trace. To disappear, it would have to be weighted, no doubt. But the awkward fact emerged that Westmacott brought a very heavy bag with him into the train (the porter gave evidence of this), and it was completely empty when examined.

"As I say, I thought Westmacott had been lucky to get off so lightly in the Resplendent affair. I didn't at all like the look of his case when I was asked to plead for him. When I went to see him I found him all broken up and in tears. He told me a long story in which he confessed to the murder of Robinson. Robinson—it was the old story—had been blackmailing him; he had evidence that it was Westmacott who attempted the murder of Smith in Cornwall. I gathered that there were other secrets behind it all which Westmacott was not anxious to go into, but it was the fear of exposure over the Smith case that made him reluctant to bring in the police against the blackmailer. Robinson had insisted on following him when he went north, afraid that he was trying to escape to the Continent by way of Leith or Aberdeen. The knowledge that he was being shadowed like this was too much for him, and he determined to get rid of his persecutor. Arranging for him to travel in the next carriage, he waited till the train was past Dalmeny, then found his man asleep, and laid him out with a piece of lead, tied that and other weights onto him as he lay there, and threw him out of the window just as the train was crossing the Forth Bridge.

"Ordinarily, when a man charged with murder tells you he is guilty you can form a pretty good guess between the two obvious alternatives—either he is telling the truth or he ought to be in an asylum. Occasionally there is a third possibility, for which the present circumstances did not seem to leave any room: he may be inculpating himself to save somebody else. I tell you, I didn't know what to make of it. The whole story seemed wrong; Westmacott was not a strong man, and what would he have done if his man had not been asleep? The chances are enormously against most men sleeping soundly on a train.

"Now, what was I to do? I felt certain the man was not mad, and I have seen many lunatics in my time. I did not, could not, believe he was really guilty. I put it to you whether, with those convictions in my mind, I was not really offering to serve the cause of truth when I urged him (as of course I did) to plead 'Not guilty.'

"He would have none of it—then. It was only a day or two later that I had an impassioned appeal to go and see him again. I found his mind entirely altered. He still stuck to his story that Robinson had been blackmailing him, but he professed to know nothing whatever about the disappearance: he thought Robinson must have either committed suicide or else staged a very clever disappearance with the sole intention of bringing him, Westmacott, to the dock. He implored me to save him from the gallows. This was too much for me; I couldn't undertake to plead for a man who didn't know from one day to the next whether he was guilty or not guilty, and gave such very lame explanations of his movements and his motives in either case. At last, when I had been at him some time, he told me a third story, which was quite different, and, as I believe, true. I shan't tell you what it was just yet. As I say, I thought, and think, it was true. But it was obvious to me from the first that it was a story you could not possibly serve up to a jury.

"There was another odd thing, which was that now, for reasons you will understand later, I did not know whether I wanted my man hanged or not. I don't know how some of you severe moralists would have formed your consciences in a situation like that. I thanked God I could fall back on a legal tradition, and I resolved that I would defend Westmacott, devoting myself single-heartedly to pointing out the weaknesses in the story, whatever it was, the prosecution would bring against him. And, gentlemen, I succeeded. I don't think I have ever had a tougher fight; there was any amount of prejudice against him among the public at large, and the jury, as usual, reflected it. But there was the solid fact that no body had been found; the open possibility that Robinson had made away with himself, or slipped off somehow when the train stopped. And, of course, the difficulty of throwing a body clear of the bridge. There was a mass of circumstantial evidence, but not a line of direct proof. Of course, you see what had happened."

McBride, who had been sitting with his head buried in his hands, lifted it slowly. "I expect I'm being a fool," he said, "but I don't believe there was any such person as Robinson. He was just Westmacott, wasn't he?"

"That's a theory to go on, at all events," admitted Sir Leonard, accepting the whisky-and-soda with which the suggestion was accompanied. "Let's hear your reasons for thinking that, and I'll put the difficulties."

"Well, as you've told the story, nobody ever saw the two men together. When Robinson was seen going out of the house, it was supposed to be Westmacott who had let him in. At the station, there was nothing to prevent Westmacott getting out of his sleeper during that last quarter of an hour, going off somewhere, and putting on the Robinson disguise, picking up fresh luggage at the cloakroom, and so making his second appearance. He made sure that the attendant should see him at Dalmeny, because he wanted everybody to think that Robinson had been thrown overboard exactly at the Forth Bridge. There was no point in making the body disappear when all the circumstances would, in any case, point to murder—unless there was no body to disappear."

"Good for you, McBride; I like to hear a man put a case well. And now let me point out the difficulties. You've got to suppose that a man who has already laboured under an awkward imputation of intended murder deliberately projects an *alter ego*—a sort of Mr Hyde—for no better purpose than to get rid of his imaginary carcass, thereby letting himself in for a second dose of suspicion. That, having done so, he first of all pretends to his counsel that he is really a murderer, and then he withdraws it all and decides to plead 'Not guilty.' Can you give a coherent explanation?"

"The man was balmy," suggested Penkridge.

"Who isn't, up to a point? But there was certainly method in poor Westmacott's madness. Shall I tell you the story he told me?"

"We'll buy it!" agreed Penkridge.

"I wonder if you could have guessed it? If so, your guesswork would have had to start from the moment at which, if you remember, Westmacott suddenly came home one day a changed man, with the shadow of something over his life. You see, he had been feeling ill for some time. He had made an appointment with a specialist, and that specialist told him the worst he had been afraid of hearing. Not only were his days numbered, but he must look forward to months of increasing pain, during which, very probably, his reason would be affected. That is the whole story; the rest just flows from it.

"Westmacott hated pain, perhaps more than most of us. He was not capable of facing great endurance, whether in action or in suffering. It didn't take him long to realize that there was only one thing for him to do—to cut his life short by suicide. He went out and bought a revolver with the necessary ammunition. He shut himself up with it, and found that his hand was that of a physical coward; it would not pull the trigger. He tried long-distance methods, bought some poison, and tried to dose himself with it. Even here he had no better success. He realized, with self-loathing, that he was a man who could not take his own life.

"It is open to you to say, if you like, that something went wrong with his brain after that, but if he had the makings of a lunatic, his was the logic of lunacy. If he could not kill himself, he must make somebody else do it for him. He had not the physique to embark on some arduous adventure: fighting, for example, or a difficult mountain climb. Bravoes cannot be hired nowadays. There was only one way he could think of inducing somebody else to kill him—*and that was to kill somebody else!* He must get himself condemned to the gallows.

"Well, as you see, he went about that in a painstaking way. He deliberately went and stayed at that appalling hotel because he knew that he would meet there the sort of people he most disliked. He found himself in luck; Smith was there, and Smith was a man who, in his view, would be all the better for extermination. Circumstances favoured him, too, in showing him a way to achieve his end. With all that reading of detective stories, you see, he had become fantastically ingenious in his conceptions of crime. He laid a trap for his victim which would make it possible for him to effect the murder by merely turning a tap, and then turning it a second time. There would be no blood, no struggle, no circumstances of violence.

"As it was, something worse happened. By mere accident, the crime of murder reduced itself to that of attempted murder, and penal servitude was no use to him. Rather sheepishly, he had to try and pass it off as a joke; all he had gained was the assurance that when he was next accused of murder, people would be apt to believe it against him. He did not attempt a second murder, which might go as wrong as the first one had gone wrong. He brought Mr Robinson into existence, and then hurried him out of existence in the way you have all heard; he had got what he wanted.

"And then, of course, the coward came out in him again, and the close prospect of the gallows frightened him more than the remote prospect of a painful death later on. He broke down, and told me the story as I have been telling it to you. And I saved him; but for the life of me I did not know whether I was doing him a benefit in trying to save him. I simply had to proceed by rule of thumb, and behave as a good advocate should."

"What became of him?" asked McBride.

"Fate stepped in, if you like to call it that. As he left the court, rather dazed with all he had gone through, he stumbled at the edge of the pavement in a crowded street, and a lorry was on the top of him before, I think, he knew what was happening. No, I saw it, and I am certain he didn't throw himself off the pavement. I don't believe he could have, either."

"There's just one comment your story suggests to me," objected Penkridge, bitter to the last. "I always thought a lawyer was not allowed to repeat the story told him in confidence by his client?"

"That is why I said that the great gift in the legal profession is imaginativeness. You see, I have been making it all up as I went along."

BLIND MAN'S HOOD

Carter Dickson

Carter Dickson was a pen-name of John Dickson Carr (1906–1977), widely regarded as the most gifted of all exponents of the locked room mystery. A native of Pennsylvania, he relocated to Britain after marrying a young Englishwoman, and launched a career as a detective novelist with a taste for the baroque. His first Great Detective, the French examining magistrate Henri Bencolin, was succeeded by Dr Gideon Fell, a rumbustious character modelled on G.K. Chesterton, whom Carr much admired. When Carr was elected to membership of the Detection Club, he was thrilled by the prospect that, as Chesterton was the Club's first President, he would at last meet his hero; sadly, Chesterton's death meant that this ambition remained unfulfilled.

As Carter Dickson, he wrote primarily about Sir Henry Merrivale, a baronet and (rather improbably) a barrister who shared Fell's penchant for solving baffling impossible crimes. He also created Colonel March, a senior cop whose exploits were ultimately brought together in a book with a title very much of its time, *The Department of Queer Complaints*. March was based on Carr's friend and fellow Detection Club member John Rhode (Major Cecil John Street, who also wrote as Miles Burton and Cecil Waye). A television series, *Colonel March of Scotland Yard*, ran for twenty-six episodes from 1955–56, with Boris Karloff cast as March and given an eyepatch to wear. This story was inspired by the unsolved Peasenhall murder case of 1902 (Carr was an aficionado of true crime), and first published in the Christmas edition of *The Sketch* in 1937.

ALTHOUGH ONE SNOWFLAKE HAD ALREADY SIFTED PAST THE lights, the great doors of the house stood open. It seemed less a snowflake than a shadow; for a bitter wind whipped after it, and the doors creaked. Inside, Rodney and Muriel Hunter could see a dingy, narrow hall paved in dull red tiles, with a Jacobean staircase at the rear. (At that time, of course, there was no dead woman lying inside.)

To find such a place in the loneliest part of the Weald of Kent—a seventeenth-century country house whose floors had grown humped and its beams scrubbed by the years—was what they had expected. Even to find electricity was not surprising. But Rodney Hunter thought he had seldom seen so many lights in one house, and Muriel had been wondering about it ever since their car turned the bend in the road. "Clearlawns" lived up to its name. It stood in the midst of a slope of flat grass, now wiry white with frost, and there was no tree or shrub within twenty yards of it. Those lights contrasted with a certain inhospitable and damp air about the house, as though the owner were compelled to keep them burning.

"But why is the front door *open*?" insisted Muriel.

In the driveway, the engine of their car coughed and died. The house was now a secret blackness of gables, emitting light at every chink, and silhouetting the stalks of the wisteria vines which climbed it. On either side of the front door were little-paned windows whose curtains had not been drawn. Towards their left they could see into a low dining-room, with table and sideboard set for a cold supper; towards their right was a darkish library moving with the reflections of a bright fire.

The sight of the fire warmed Rodney Hunter, but it made him feel guilty. They were very late. At five o'clock, without fail, he had promised Jack Bannister, they would be at "Clearlawns" to inaugurate the Christmas party.

Engine trouble in leaving London was one thing; idling at a country pub along the way, drinking hot ale and listening to the wireless sing carols until a sort of Dickensian jollity stole into you, was something else. But both he and Muriel were young; they were very fond of each other and of things in general; and they had worked themselves into a glow of Christmas, which— as they stood before the creaking doors of "Clearlawns"—grew oddly cool.

There was no real reason, Rodney thought, to feel disquiet. He hoisted their luggage, including a big box of presents for Jack and Molly's children, out of the rear of the car. That his footsteps should sound loud on the gravel was only natural. He put his head into the doorway and whistled. Then he began to bang the knocker. Its sound seemed to seek out every corner of the house and then come back like a questing dog; but there was no response.

"I'll tell you something else," he said. "There's nobody in the house."

Muriel ran up the three steps to stand beside him. She had drawn her fur coat close around her, and her face was bright with cold.

"But that's impossible!" she said. "I mean, even if they're out, the servants—! Molly told me she keeps a cook and two maids. Are you sure we've got the right place?"

"Yes. The name's on the gate, and there's no other house within a mile."

With the same impulse they craned their necks to look through the windows of the dining-room on the left. Cold fowl on the sideboard, a great bowl of chestnuts; and, now they could see it, another good fire, before which stood a chair with a piece of knitting put aside on it. Rodney tried the knocker again, vigorously, but the sound was all wrong. It was as though they were even more lonely in that core of light, with the east wind rushing across the Weald, and the door creaking again.

"I suppose we'd better go in," said Rodney. He added, with a lack of Christmas spirit: "Here, this is a devil of a trick! What do you think has happened? I'll swear that fire has been made up in the last fifteen minutes."

He stepped into the hall and set down the bags. As he was turning to close the door, Muriel put her hand on his arm.

"I say, Rod. Do you think you'd better close it?"

"Why not?"

"I—I don't know."

"The place is getting chilly enough as it is," he pointed out, unwilling to admit that the same thought had occurred to him. He closed both doors and shot their bar into place; and, at the same moment, a girl came out of the door to the library on the right.

She was such a pleasant-faced girl that they both felt a sense of relief. Why she had not answered the knocking had ceased to be a question; she filled a void. She was pretty, not more than twenty-one or two, and had an air of primness which made Rodney Hunter vaguely associate her with a governess or a secretary, though Jack Bannister had never mentioned any such person. She was plump, but with a curiously narrow waist; and she wore brown. Her brown hair was neatly parted, and her brown eyes—long eyes, which might have given a hint of secrecy or curious smiles if they had not been so placid—looked concerned. In one hand she carried what looked like a small white bag of linen or cotton. And she spoke with a dignity which did not match her years.

"I am most terribly sorry," she told them. "I *thought* I heard someone, but I was so busy that I could not be sure. Will you forgive me?"

She smiled. Hunter's private view was that his knocking had been loud enough to wake the dead; but he murmured conventional things. As though conscious of some faint incongruity about the white bag in her hand, she held it up.

"For Blind Man's Bluff," she explained. "They do cheat so, I'm afraid, and not only the children. If one uses an ordinary handkerchief tied round the eyes, they always manage to get a corner loose. But if you take this, and you put it fully over a person's head, and you tie it round the neck"—a sudden gruesome image occurred to Rodney Hunter—"then it works so much better, don't you think?" Her eyes seemed to turn inward, and to grow absent. "But I must not keep you talking here. You are—?"

"My name is Hunter. This is my wife. I'm afraid we've arrived late, but I understood Mr Bannister was expecting—"

"He did not tell you?" asked the girl in brown.

"Tell me what?"

"Everyone here, including the servants, is always out of the house at this hour on this particular date. It is the custom; I believe it has been the custom for more than sixty years. There is some sort of special church service."

Rodney Hunter's imagination had been devising all sorts of

fantastic explanations: the first of them being that this demure lady had murdered the members of the household, and was engaged in disposing of the bodies. What put this nonsensical notion into his head he could not tell, unless it was his own profession of detective story writing. But he felt relieved to hear a commonplace explanation. Then the woman spoke again.

"Of course, it is a pretext, really. The rector, that dear man, invented it all those years ago to save embarrassment. What happened here had nothing to do with the murder, since the dates were so different; and I suppose most people have forgotten now why the tenants *do* prefer to stay away during seven and eight o'clock on Christmas Eve. I doubt if Mrs Bannister even knows the real reason, though I should imagine Mr Bannister must know it. But what happens here cannot be very pleasant, and it wouldn't do to have the children see it—would it?"

Muriel spoke with such sudden directness that her husband knew she was afraid. "Who are you?" Muriel said. "And what on earth are you talking about?"

"I am quite sane, really," their hostess assured them, with a smile that was half-cheery and half-coy. "I dare say it must be all very confusing to you, poor dear. But I am forgetting my duties. Please come in and sit down before the fire, and let me offer you something to drink."

She took them into the library on the right, going ahead with a walk that was like a bounce, and looking over her shoulder out of those long eyes. The library was a long, low room with beams. The windows towards the road were uncurtained; but those in the side-wall, where a faded redbrick fireplace stood,, were bay windows with draperies closed across them. As their hostess put them before the fire, Hunter could have sworn he saw one of the draperies move.

"You need not worry about it," she assured him, following his glance towards the bay. "Even if you looked in there, you might not see anything now. I believe some gentleman did try it once, a long time ago. He stayed in the house for a wager. But when he pulled the curtain back, he did not see anything in the bay—at least, anything quite. He felt some hair, and it moved. That is why they have so many lights nowadays."

Muriel had sat down on a sofa, and was lighting a cigarette: to the rather prim disapproval of their hostess, Hunter thought.

"May we have a hot drink?" Muriel asked crisply. "And then, if you don't mind, we might walk over and meet the Bannisters coming from church."

"Oh, please don't do that!" cried the other. She had been standing by the fireplace, her hands folded and turned outwards. Now she ran across to sit down beside Muriel; and the swiftness of her movement, no less than the touch of her hand on Muriel's arm, made the latter draw back.

Hunter was now completely convinced that their hostess was out of her head. Why she held such fascination for him, though, he could not understand. In her eagerness to keep them there, the girl had come upon a new idea. On a table behind the sofa, bookends held a row of modern novels. Conspicuously displayed—probably due to Molly Bannister's tact—were two of Rodney Hunter's detective stories. The girl put a finger on them.

"May I ask if you wrote these?"

He admitted it.

"Then," she said with sudden composure, "it would probably interest you to hear about the murder. It was a most perplexing business, you know; the police could make nothing of it, and no one ever has been able to solve it." An arresting eye fixed on his.

"It happened out in the hall there. A poor woman was killed where there was no one to kill her, and no one could have done it. But she was murdered."

Hunter started to get up from his chair; then he changed his mind, and sat down again. "Go on," he said.

"You must forgive me if I am a little uncertain about dates," she urged. "I think it was in the early eighteen-seventies, and I am sure it was in early February—because of the snow. It was a bad winter then; the farmers' livestock all died. My people have been bred up in the district for years, and I know that. The house here was much as it is now, except that there was none of this lighting (only paraffin lamps, poor girl!); and you were obliged to pump up what water you wanted; and people read the newspaper quite through, and discussed it for days.

"The people were a little different to look at, too. I am sure I do not understand why we think beards are so strange nowadays; they seem to think that men who had beards never had any emotions. But even young men wore them then, and looked handsome enough. There was a newly married couple living in this house at the time: at least, they had been married only the summer before. They were named Edward and Jane Waycross, and it was considered a good match everywhere.

"Edward Waycross did not have a beard, but he had bushy side-whiskers which he kept curled. He was not a handsome man, either, being somewhat dry and hard-favoured; but he was a religious man, and a good man, and an excellent man of business, they say: a manufacturer of agricultural implements at Hawkhurst. He had determined that Jane Anders (as she was) would make him a good wife, and I dare say she did. The girl had several suitors. Although

Mr Waycross was the best match, I know it surprised people a little when she accepted him, because, she was thought to have been fond of another man—a more striking man, whom many of the young girls were after. This was Jeremy Wilkes: who came of a very good family, but was considered wicked. He was no younger than Mr Waycross, but he had a great black beard, and wore white waistcoats with gold chains, drove a gig. Of course, there had been gossip, but that was because Jane Anders was considered pretty."

Their hostess had been sitting back against the sofa, quietly folding the little white bag with one hand, and speaking in a prim voice. Now she did something which turned her hearers cold.

You have probably seen the same thing done many times. She had been touching her cheek lightly with the fingers of the other hand. In doing so, she touched the flesh at the corner under her lower eyelid, and accidentally drew down the corner of that eyelid—which should have exposed the red part of the inner lid at the corner of the eye. It was not red. It was of a sickly pale colour.

"In the course of his business dealings," she went on, "Mr Waycross had often to go to London, and usually he was obliged to remain overnight. But Jane Waycross was not afraid to remain alone in the house. She had a good servant, a staunch old woman, and a good dog. Even so, Mr Waycross commended her for her courage."

The girl smiled. "On the night I wish to tell you of, in February, Mr Waycross was absent. Unfortunately, too, the old servant was absent; she had been called away as a midwife to attend her cousin, and Jane Waycross had allowed her to go. This was known in the village, since all such affairs are well known, and some uneasiness was felt—this house being isolated, as you know. But she was not afraid.

"It was a very cold night, with a heavy fall of snow which had stopped about nine o'clock. You must know, beyond doubt, that poor Jane Waycross was alive after it had stopped snowing. It must have been nearly half past nine when a Mr Moody—a very good and sober man who lived in Hawkhurst—was driving home along the road past this house. As you know, it stands in the middle of a great bare stretch of lawn; and you can see the house clearly from the road. Mr Moody saw poor Jane at the window of one of the upstairs bedrooms, with a candle in her hand, closing the shutters. But he was not the only witness who saw her alive.

"On that same evening, Mr Wilkes (the handsome gentleman I spoke to you of a moment ago) had been at a tavern in the village of Five Ashes with Dr Sutton, the local doctor, and a racing gentleman named Pawley. At about half past eleven they started to drive home in Mr Wilkes's gig to Cross-in-Hand. I am afraid they had been drinking, but they were all in their sober senses. The landlord of the tavern remembered the time because he had stood in the doorway to watch the gig, which had fine yellow wheels, go spanking away as though there were no snow; and Mr Wilkes in one of the new round hats with a curly brim.

"There was a bright moon. 'And no danger,' Dr Sutton always said afterwards; 'shadows of trees and fences as clear as though a silhouette cutter had made 'em for sixpence.' But when they were passing this house Mr Wilkes pulled up sharp. There was a bright light in the window of one of the downstairs rooms—this room, in fact. They sat out there looking round the hood of the gig, and wondering.

"Mr Wilkes spoke: 'I don't like this,' he said. 'You know, gentlemen, that Waycross is still in London; and the lady in question is in the habit of retiring early. I am going up there to find out if anything is wrong.'

"With that he jumped out of the gig, his black beard jutting out and his breath smoking. He said: 'And if it is a burglar, then, by Something, gentlemen'—I will not repeat the word he used—'by Something, gentlemen, I'll settle him.' He walked through the gate and up to the house—they could follow every step he made—and looked into the windows of this room here. Presently he returned looking relieved (they could see him by the light of the gig lamps), but wiping the moisture off his forehead.

"'It is all right,' he said to them; 'Waycross has come home. But, by Something, gentlemen, he is growing thinner these days, or it is shadows.'

"Then he told them what he had seen. If you look through the front windows—there—you can look sideways and see out through the doorway into the main hall. He said he had seen Mrs Waycross standing in the hall with her back to the staircase, wearing a blue dressing-wrap over her nightgown, and her hair down round her shoulders. Standing in front of her, with his back to Mr Wilkes, was a tallish, thin man like Mr Waycross, with a long greatcoat and a tall hat like Mr Waycross's. *She* was carrying either a candle or a lamp; and he remembered how the tall hat seemed to wag back and forth, as though the man were talking to her or putting out his hands towards her. For he said he could not see the woman's face.

"Of course, it was not Mr Waycross; but how were they to know that?

"At about seven o'clock next morning, Mrs Randall, the old servant, returned. (A fine boy had been born to her cousin the night before.) Mrs Randall came home through the white dawn and the white snow, and found the house all locked up. She could get no answer to her knocking. Being a woman of great resolution, she eventually broke a window and got in. But, when she saw what was in the front hall, she went out screaming for help.

"Poor Jane was past help. I know I should not speak of these things; but I must. She was lying on her face in the hall. From the waist down her body was much charred and—unclothed, you know, because fire had burnt away most of the nightgown and the dressing-wrap. The tiles of the hall were soaked with blood and paraffin oil, the oil having come from a broken lamp with a thick blue-silk shade which was lying a little distance away. Near it was a china candlestick with a candle. This fire had also charred a part of the panelling of the wall, and a part of the staircase. Fortunately, the floor is of brick tiles, and there had not been much paraffin left in the lamp, or the house would have been set afire.

"But she had not died from burns alone. Her throat had been cut with a deep slash from some very sharp blade. But she had been alive for a while to feel both things, for she had crawled forward on her hands while she was burning. It was a cruel death, a horrible death for a soft person like that."

There was a pause. The expression on the face of the narrator, the plump girl in the brown dress, altered slightly. So did the expression of her eyes. She was sitting beside Muriel; and moved a little closer.

"Of course, the police came. I do not understand such things, I am afraid, but they found that the house had not been robbed. They also noticed the odd thing I have mentioned, that there was both a lamp *and* a candle in a candlestick near her. The lamp came from Mr and Mrs Waycross's bedroom upstairs, and so did the candlestick: there were no other lamps or candles downstairs except the lamps waiting to be filled next morning in the back kitchen. But the police thought she would not have come downstairs carrying both the lamp *and* the candle as well.

"She must have brought the lamp, because that was broken. When the murderer took hold of her, they thought, she had dropped the lamp, and it went out; the paraffin spilled, but did not catch fire. Then this man in the tall hat, to finish his work after he had cut her throat, went upstairs, and got a candle, and set fire to the spilled oil. I am stupid at these things; but even I should have guessed that this must mean someone familiar with the house. Also, if she came downstairs, it must have been to let someone in at the front door; and that could not have been a burglar.

"You may be sure all the gossips were like police from the start, even when the police hemm'd and haw'd, because they knew Mrs Waycross must have opened the door to a man who was not her husband. And immediately they found an indication of this, in the mess that the fire and blood had made in the hall. Some distance away from poor Jane's body there was a medicine-bottle, such as chemists use. I think it had been broken in two pieces; and on one intact piece they found sticking some fragments of a letter that had not been quite burned. It was in a man's handwriting, not her husband's, and they made out enough of it to understand. It was full of—expressions of love, you know, and it made an appointment to meet her there on that night."

Rodney Hunter, as the girl paused, felt impelled to ask a question.

"Did they know whose handwriting it was?"

"It was Jeremy Wilkes's," replied the other simply. "Though they never proved that, never more than slightly suspected it, and the circumstances did not bear it out. In fact, a knife stained with blood was actually found in Mr Wilkes's possession. But the police never brought it to anything, poor souls. For, you see, not Mr Wilkes—or anyone else in the world—could possibly have done the murder."

"I don't understand that," said Hunter, rather sharply.

"Forgive me if I am stupid about telling things," urged their hostess in a tone of apology. She seemed to be listening to the chimney growl under a cold sky, and listening with hard, placid eyes. "But even the village gossips could tell that. When Mrs Randall came here to the house on that morning, both the front and the back doors were locked and securely bolted on the inside. All the windows were locked on the inside. If you will look at the fastenings in this dear place, you will know what that means.

"But, bless you, that was the least of it! I told you about the snow. The snowfall had stopped at nine o'clock in the evening, hours and hours before Mrs Waycross was murdered. When the police came, there were only two separate sets of footprints in the great unmarked half-acre of snow round the house. One set belonged to Mr Wilkes, who had come up and looked in through the window the night before. The other belonged to Mrs Randall. The police could follow and explain both sets of tracks; but there were no other tracks at all, and no one was hiding in the house.

"Of course, it was absurd to suspect Mr Wilkes. It was not only that he told a perfectly straight story about the man in the tall hat; but both Dr Sutton and Mr Pawley, who drove back with him from Five Ashes, were there to swear he could not have done it. You understand, he came no closer to the house than the windows of this room. They could watch every step he made in the moonlight, and they did. Afterwards he drove home with Dr Sutton, and slept there; or, I should say, they continued their terrible drinking until daylight. It is true that they found in his possession a knife with blood on it, but he explained that he had used the knife to gut a rabbit.

"It was the same with poor Mrs Randall, who had been up all night about her midwife's duties, though naturally it was even more absurd to think of *her*. But there were no other footprints at all, either coming to or going from the house, in all that stretch of snow; and all the ways in or out were locked on the inside."

It was Muriel who spoke then, in a voice that tried to be crisp, but wavered in spite of her. "Are you telling us that all this is true?" she demanded.

"I am teasing you a little, my dear," said the other. "But, really and truly, it all did happen. Perhaps I will show you in a moment."

"I suppose it was really the husband who did it?" asked Muriel in a bored tone.

"Poor Mr Waycross!" said their hostess tenderly. "He spent that night in a temperance hotel near Charing Cross Station, as he always did, and, of course, he never left it. When he learned about his wife's duplicity"—again Hunter thought she was going to pull down a corner of her eyelid—"it nearly drove him out of his mind, poor fellow. I think he gave up agricultural machinery and took to preaching, but I am not sure. I know he left the district soon afterwards, and before he left he insisted on burning the mattress of their bed. It was a dreadful scandal."

"But in that case," insisted Hunter, "who did kill her? And, if there were no footprints and all the doors were locked, how did the murderer come or go? Finally, if all this happened in February, what does it have to do with people being out of the house on Christmas Eve?"

"Ah, that is the real story. That is what I meant to tell you."

She grew very subdued.

"It must have been very interesting to watch the people alter and grow older, or find queer paths, in the years afterwards. For, of course, nothing did happen as yet. The police presently gave it all up; for decency's sake it was allowed to rest. There was a new pump built in the market square; and the news of the Prince of Wales's going to India in '75 to talk about; and presently a new family came to live at 'Clearlawns,' and began to raise their children. The trees and the rains in summer were just the same, you know. It must have been seven or eight years before anything happened, for Jane Waycross was very patient.

"Several of the people had died in the meantime. Mrs Randall had, in a fit of quinsy; and so had Dr Sutton, but that was a great mercy, because he fell by the way when he was going out to perform an amputation with too much of the drink in him. But Mr Pawley had prospered—and, above all, so had Mr Wilkes. He had become an even finer figure of a man, they tell me, as he drew near middle age. When he married he gave up all his loose habits. Yes, he married; it was the Tinsley heiress, Miss Linshaw, whom he had been courting at the time of the murder; and I have heard that poor Jane Waycross, even after *she* was married to Mr Waycross, used to bite her pillow at night because she was so horribly jealous of Miss Linshaw.

"Mr Wilkes had always been tall, and now he was finely stout. He always wore frock-coats. Though he had lost most of his hair, his beard was full and curly; he had twinkling black eyes, and twinkling ruddy cheeks, and a bluff voice. All the children ran to him. They say he broke as many feminine hearts as before. At any wholesome entertainment he was always the first to lead the cotillion or applaud the fiddler, and I do not know what hostesses would have done without him.

"On Christmas Eve, then—remember, I am not sure of the date—the Fentons gave a Christmas party. The Fentons were the very nice family who had taken this house afterwards, you know. There was to be no dancing, but all the old games. Naturally, Mr Wilkes was the first of all to be invited, and the first to accept; for everything was all smoothed away by time, like the wrinkles in last year's counterpane; and what's past *is* past, or so they say. They had decorated the house with holly and mistletoe, and guests began to arrive as early as two in the afternoon.

"I had all this from Mrs Fenton's aunt (one of the Warwickshire Abbotts), who was actually staying here at the time. In spite of such a festal season, the preparations had not been going at all well that day, though such preparations usually did. Miss Abbott complained that there was a nasty earthy smell in the house. It was a dark and raw day, and the chimneys did not seem to draw as well as they should. What is more, Mrs Fenton cut her finger when she was carving the cold fowl, because she said one of the children had been hiding behind the window curtains in here, and peeping out at her; she was very angry. But Mr Fenton, who was going about the house in his carpet slippers before the arrival of the guests, called her 'Mother' and said that it was Christmas.

"It is certainly true that they forgot all about this when the fun of the games began. Such squealings you never heard!—or so I am told. Foremost of all at Bobbing for Apples or Nuts in May was Mr Jeremy Wilkes. He stood, gravely paternal, in the midst of everything, with his ugly wife beside him, and stroked his beard. He saluted each of the ladies on the cheek under the mistletoe; there was also some scampering to salute him; and, though he *did* remain for longer than was necessary behind the window curtains with the younger Miss Twigelow, his wife only smiled. There was only one unpleasant incident, soon forgotten. Towards dusk a great gusty wind began to come up, with the chimneys smoking worse than usual. It being nearly dark, Mr Fenton said it was time to fetch in the Snapdragon Bowl, and watch it flame. You know the game? It is a great bowl of lighted spirit, and you must thrust in your hand and pluck out a raisin from the bottom without scorching your fingers. Mr Fenton carried it in on a tray in the half-darkness; it was flickering with that bluish flame you have seen on Christmas puddings. Miss Abbott said that once, in carrying it, he started and turned round. She said that for a second she thought there was a face looking over his shoulder, and it wasn't a nice face.

"Later in the evening, when the children were sleepy and there was tissue-paper scattered all over the house, the grown-ups began their games in earnest. Someone suggested Blind Man's Bluff. They were mostly using the hall and this room here, as having more space than the dining-room. Various members of the party were blindfolded with the men's handkerchiefs; but there was a dreadful amount of cheating. Mr Fenton grew quite annoyed about it, because the ladies almost always caught Mr Wilkes when they could; Mr Wilkes was laughing and perspiring heartily, and his great cravat with the silver pin had almost come loose.

"To make it certain nobody could cheat, Mr Fenton got a little white linen bag—like this one. It was the pillow-cover off the baby's cot, really; and he said nobody could look through that if it were tied over the head.

"I should explain that they had been having some trouble with the lamp in this room. Mr Fenton said: 'Confound it, mother, what is wrong with that lamp? Turn up the wick, will you?' It was really quite a good lamp from Spence and Minstead's, and should not have burned so dull as it did. In the confusion, while Mrs Fenton was trying to make the light better, and he was looking over his shoulder at her, Mr Fenton had been rather absently fastening the bag on the head of the last person caught. He has said since that he did not notice who it was. No one else noticed, either, the light being so dim and there being such a large number of people. It seemed to be a girl in a broad bluish kind of dress, standing over near the door.

"Perhaps you know how people act when they have just been blindfolded in this game. First they usually stand very still, as though they were smelling or sensing in which direction to go. Sometimes they make a sudden jump, or sometimes they begin to shuffle gently forward. Everyone noticed what an air of *purpose* there seemed to be about this person whose face was covered; she went forward very slowly, and seemed to crouch down a bit.

"It began to move towards Mr Wilkes in very short but quick little jerks, the white bag bobbing on its face. At this time Mr Wilkes was sitting at the end of the table, laughing, with his face pink above the beard, and a glass of our Kentish cider in his hand. I want you to imagine this room as being very dim, and much more cluttered, what with all the tassels they had on the furniture then; and the high-piled hair of the ladies, too. The hooded person got to the edge of the table. It began to edge along towards Mr Wilkes's chair; and then it jumped.

"Mr Wilkes got up and skipped (yes, skipped) out of its way, laughing. It waited quietly, after which it went, in the same slow way, towards him again. It nearly got him again, by the edge of the potted plant. All this time it did not say anything, you understand, although everyone was applauding it and crying encouraging advice. It kept its head down. Miss Abbott says she began to notice an unpleasant faint smell of burnt cloth or something worse, which turned her half ill. By the time the hooded person came stooping clear across the room, as certainly as though it could see him, Mr Wilkes was not laughing any longer.

"In the corner by one bookcase, he said out loud: 'I'm tired of this silly, rotten game; go away, do you hear?' Nobody there had ever heard him speak like that, in such a loud, wild way, but they laughed and thought it must be the Kentish cider. 'Go away!' cried Mr Wilkes again, and began to strike at it with his fist. All this time, Miss Abbott says, she had observed his face gradually changing. He dodged again, very pleasant and nimble for such a big man, but with the perspiration running down his face. Back across the room he went again, with it following him; and he cried out something that most naturally shocked them all inexpressibly.

"He screamed out: 'For God's sake, Fenton, take it off me!'

"And for the last time the thing jumped.

"They were over near the curtains of that bay window, which were drawn as they are now. Miss Twigelow, who was nearest, says that Mr Wilkes could not have seen anything, because the white bag was still drawn over the woman's head. The only thing she noticed was that at the lower part of the bag, where the face must have been, there was a curious kind of discoloration, a stain of some sort which had not been there before: something seemed to be seeping through. Mr Wilkes fell back between the curtains, with the hooded person after him, and screamed again. There was a kind of thrashing noise in or behind the curtains; then they fell straight again, and everything grew quiet.

"Now, our Kentish cider is very strong, and for a moment Mr Fenton did not know what to think. He tried to laugh at it, but the laugh did not sound well. Then he went over to the curtains, calling out gruffly to them to come out of there and not play the fool. But, after he had looked inside the curtains, he turned round very sharply and asked the rector to get the ladies out of the room. This was done, but Miss Abbott often said that she had one quick peep inside. Though the bay windows were locked on the inside, Mr Wilkes was now alone on the window seat. She could see his beard sticking up, and the blood. He was dead, of course. But, since he had murdered Jane Waycross, I sincerely think that he deserved to die."

For several seconds the two listeners did not move. She had all too successfully conjured up this room in the late seventies, whose stuffiness still seemed to pervade it now.

"But look here!" protested Hunter, when he could fight down an inclination to get out of the room quickly. "You say he killed her after all? And yet you told us he had an absolute alibi. You said he never went closer to the house than the windows…"

"No more he did, my dear," said the other.

"He was courting the Linshaw heiress at the time," she resumed; "and Miss Linshaw was a very proper young lady who would have been horrified if she had heard about him and Jane Waycross. She would have broken off the match, naturally. But poor Jane Waycross meant her to hear. She was much in love with Mr Wilkes, and she was going to tell the whole matter publicly: Mr Wilkes had been trying to persuade her not to do so."

"But—"

"Oh, don't you see what happened?" cried the other in a pettish tone. "It is so dreadfully simple. I am not clever at these things, but I should have seen it in a moment: even if I did not already know. I told you everything so that you should be able to guess.

"When Mr Wilkes and Dr Sutton and Mr Pawley drove past here in the gig that night, they saw a bright light burning in the windows of this room. I told you that. But the police never wondered, as anyone should, what caused that light. Jane Waycross never came into this room, as you know; she was out in the hall, carrying either a lamp or a candle. But that lamp in the thick blue-silk shade, held out there in the hall, would not have caused a bright light to shine through this room and illuminate it. Neither would a tiny candle; it is absurd. And I told you there were no other lamps in the house except some empty ones waiting to be filled in the back kitchen. There is only one thing they could have seen. They saw the great blaze of the paraffin oil round Jane Waycross's body.

"Didn't I tell you it was dreadfully simple? Poor Jane was upstairs waiting for her lover. From the upstairs window she saw Mr Wilkes's gig drive along the road in the moonlight, and she did not know there were other men in it; she thought he was alone. She came downstairs—

"It is an awful thing that the police did not think more about that broken medicine bottle lying in the hall, the large bottle that was broken in just two long pieces. She must have had a use for it; and, of course, she had. You knew that the oil in the lamp was almost exhausted, although there was a great blaze round the body. When poor Jane came downstairs, she was carrying the unlighted lamp in one hand; in the other hand she was carrying a lighted candle, and an old medicine bottle containing paraffin oil. When she got downstairs, she meant to fill the lamp from the medicine bottle, and then light it with the candle.

"But she was too eager to get downstairs, I am afraid. When she was more than half way down, hurrying, that long nightgown tripped her. She pitched forward down the stairs on her face. The medicine-bottle broke on the tiles under her, and poured a lake of paraffin round her body. Of course, the lighted candle set the paraffin blazing when it fell; but that was not all. One intact side of that broken bottle, long and sharp and cleaner than any blade, cut into her throat when she fell on the smashed bottle. She was not quite stunned by the fall. When she felt herself burning, and the blood almost as hot, she tried to save herself. She tried to crawl forward on her hands, forward into the hall, away from the blood and oil and fire.

"That was what Mr Wilkes really saw when he looked in through the window.

"You see, he had been unable to get rid of the two fuddled friends, who insisted on clinging to him and drinking with him. He had been obliged to drive them home. If he could not go to 'Clearlawns' now, he wondered how at least he could leave a message; and the light in the window gave him an excuse.

"He saw pretty Jane propped up on her hands in the hall, looking out at him beseechingly while the blue flame ran up and turned yellow. You might have thought he would have pitied, for she loved him very much. Her wound was not really a deep wound. If he had broken into the house at that moment, he might have saved her life. But he preferred to let her die: because now she would make no public scandal and spoil his chances with the rich Miss Linshaw. That was why he returned to his friends and told a lie about a murderer in a tall hat. It is why, in heaven's truth, he murdered her himself. But when he returned to his friends, I do not wonder that they saw him mopping his forehead. You know now how Jane Waycross came back for him, presently."

There was another heavy silence.

The girl got to her feet, with a sort of bouncing motion which was as suggestive as it was vaguely familiar. It was as though she were about to run. She stood there, a trifle crouched, in her prim brown dress, so oddly narrow at the waist after an old-fashioned pattern; and in the play of light on her face Rodney Hunter fancied that its prettiness was only a shell.

"The same thing happened afterwards, on some Christmas Eves," she explained. "They played Blind Man's Bluff over again. That is why people who live here do not care to risk it nowadays. It happens at a quarter-past seven—"

Hunter stared at the curtains. "But it was a quarter past seven when we got here!" he said. "It must now be—"

"Oh, yes," said the girl, and her eyes brimmed over. "You see, I told you you had nothing to fear; it was all over then. But that is not why I thank you. I begged you to stay, and you did. You have listened to me, as no one else would. And now I have told it at last, and now I think both of us can sleep."

Not a fold stirred or altered in the dark curtains that closed the window bay; yet, as though a blurred lens had come into focus, they now seemed innocent and devoid of harm. You could have put a Christmas tree there. Rodney Hunter, with Muriel following his gaze, walked across and threw back the curtains. He saw a quiet window-seat covered with chintz, and the rising moon beyond the window. When he turned round, the girl in the old-fashioned dress was not there. But the front doors were open again, for he could feel a current of air blowing through the house.

With his arm round Muriel, who was white-faced, he went out into the hall. They did not look long at the scorched and beaded stains at the foot of the panelling, for even the scars of fire seemed gentle now. Instead, they stood in the doorway looking out, while the house threw its great blaze of light across the frosty Weald. It was a welcoming light. Over the rise of a hill, black dots trudging in the frost showed that Jack Bannister's party was returning; and they could hear the sound of voices carrying far. They heard one of the party carelessly singing a Christmas carol for glory and joy, and the laughter of children coming home.

PAUL TEMPLE'S WHITE CHRISTMAS

Francis Durbridge

Francis Henry Durbridge (1912–1998) became a household name as creator of Paul Temple, the debonair amateur detective to whom the hapless Sir Graham Forbes of Scotland Yard was forever turning for help when confounded by bewildering crime. Durbridge's radio serials with their trademark cliff-hanger endings and multiple plot twists, became hugely popular in the Thirties, and in the post-war era; he became equally celebrated for a long run of television serials, including *Melissa*, *Bat out of Hell*, and *A Game of Murder*. There were four Paul Temple films, and other movies based on his work included *The Vicious Circle* (1957).

As if all that wasn't enough, there was a Paul Temple comic strip that enjoyed a long run in various newspapers, while a television series, *Paul Temple*, with the urbane Francis Matthews well cast as the gentlemanly sleuth, clocked up fifty-two episodes from 1969–1971; the television scripts and most of the comic strips were not, however, based on Durbridge's serials. In the latter part of his career, he concentrated on writing for the stage, and several of his mystery plays, starting with *Suddenly at Home* (1971), became West End hits.

As a writer, Durbridge's strengths lay in building suspense, pace, and dialogue, and this helps to explain why his finest work was for radio and television. Writing prose narratives formed a relatively minor part of his output. The majority of his books were, in reality, novelizations; a rare exception was the stand-alone thriller *Back Room Girl* (1950). This little story first appeared in *Radio Times* on 20 December 1946.

S TEVE STOPPED TALKING ABOUT SWITZERLAND, TORE UP THE
Winter Sports brochure, and went out shopping. She said that
she would meet Temple at the Penguin Club at a quarter past four.
"I shan't be a minute later than four-fifteen," she said gaily.

That was two hours ago.

It was now precisely twenty-seven-and-a-half minutes past five
and Temple was still waiting. He sat with his back to the bar staring
out at the rain and drinking a dry martini. Cecil, the bar-tender,
was talking about *The Gregory Affair*. He'd been talking about *The
Gregory Affair* for thirty-seven minutes. Temple was tired. He was
tired of waiting, of the Club, of Cecil, of hearing about *The Gregory
Affair,* and—most of all—he was tired of the rain. He was almost
beginning to wish that he'd taken Steve's advice about Switzerland.

It had just gone half-past five when Steve arrived. She put her
parcels down on the high stool and smiled at Cecil. "It's filthy
weather, Paul—don't you wish we'd gone to Switzerland?"

Temple brought his wristlet watch dangerously near her veil.
He said: "It's five-thirty, you're just an hour and a quarter late,
Steve!"

"Yes. I bumped into Freda Gwenn and she never stopped talking. The poor dear's wildly excited."

"Why is she excited?"

"She's going to Switzerland for Christmas and…"

Temple took Steve by the arm, said goodbye to Cecil, and
picked up the parcels.

They stood for a moment in the doorway looking out at the rain. "If there's anything I like better than a good old English winter," said Steve, "it's a good old English summer."

Temple said: "What do you expect at this time of the year?"

"I know what I'd like! I'd like…"

"You'd like to slide on your posterior all day," said Temple, "and dance your feet off all night."

Steve said: "You *are* in a pleasant mood, darling! What you need is plenty of fresh air and exercise." She was thinking of St Moritz and the Palace Hotel skating rink.

Temple nodded. "It's a good idea, we'll walk back to the flat."

It was still raining but they walked.

When they got back to the flat there was a note from Charlie. It was on the small table in the hall and like most of Charlie's notes it was brief and to the point. *"Off to the Palais de Danse. Sir Graham rang up—he's ringing again. Be good. Charlie."*

Temple didn't care very much for the "be good" touch, but it was typical of Charlie. It was an hour later when Sir Graham telephoned. Steve was in the bathroom.

"You remember that Luxembourg counterfeit business you helped us with last year?" the Commissioner said. Temple remembered it only too well. For one thing the leader of the organization—a man called Howell—had mysteriously disappeared.

"Yes. I remember it, Sir Graham. Don't tell me you've caught up with the elusive Mr Howell?"

"We haven't, but it rather looks as if the Swiss people have. They arrested a man they believe to be Howell just over twenty-four hours ago."

"What happened?"

"Apparently this fellow had managed to get some sort of an organization together and was ready to start work at Grindelwald. By a sheer stroke of genius the Swiss authorities caught up with him."

"Did they get the rest of the organization?"

"No, I'm afraid they didn't." Forbes laughed. "As a matter of fact they're not absolutely certain that they've got Howell."

"What do you mean?"

Forbes said: "Well, the Swiss people seem to think that while Howell was lying low after the Luxembourg business he had a fairly drastic facial operation: you know the sort of thing—plastic surgery."

Temple could hear Steve splashing about in the bathroom. He said in a low voice: "Do I come into this, Sir Graham?"

"I'm rather afraid you do, Temple," said Sir Graham. "The Swiss authorities want somebody to go out there and identify Howell. Preferably somebody who worked on the Luxembourg business."

"Where is Howell?"

"He was arrested at Grindelwald but they've taken him to Interlaken. I rather gather the police are a little frightened that the rest of the gang might try to rescue him."

Temple said: "When do you expect us to leave?"

He heard Forbes chuckling at the other end of the wire.

"I thought Steve would have to come into the picture!" he said. "You leave tomorrow morning on the eleven o'clock 'plane. You'll land at Berne and go on to Interlaken by train."

Temple said goodbye, put down the receiver, lit a cigarette, and sat watching the bathroom door. After a little while the door opened and Steve appeared. She was wearing a grey negligé. Temple had always thought it was a very nice negligé.

Temple said: "I've got a surprise for you. I'll give you three guesses."

Steve said: "It's stopped raining."

"No."

"M.G.M. have bought your last novel?"

"No."

Steve brushed her hair with the towel. "My intuition isn't working tonight I give up."

Temple said: "It looks like being a White Christmas after all. We leave for Berne tomorrow morning."

The 'plane landed at the airport and Temple and Steve made their way towards the Customs. Temple took one look at the weather. It was raining. "If there's one thing I like better than a good old Swiss winter," he said, "it's a good old Swiss summer."

Steve laughed and took him by the arm. There was a man waiting for them at the barrier. A tall, clean-shaven, rather distinguished looking man in a dark brown overcoat.

He touched his hat to Steve and addressed Temple:

"Mr Paul Temple?"

"Yes?"

"My name is Velquez, sir. Inspector Velquez. I've been asked by the authorities to drive you into Berne."

Temple eyed him cautiously, and said: "Why Berne, Inspector?"

The man smiled. "We've taken Howell to Berne, sir. We thought it might save time. My car is at your disposal."

Temple said: "Well, Inspector, my instructions are to proceed by train to Interlaken. I think I ought to get this change of programme confirmed by your superior."

Velquez smiled. He had quite a pleasant smile. "Then I advise you to telephone through to headquarters," he said, "you'll find the telephone in the waiting room and the number is Interlaken 9-8974. Ask for M. Dumas."

Steve stayed with Velquez while Temple telephoned.

It was apparently M. Dumas himself who answered the telephone. He was extremely affable and rather amused by the precaution Paul Temple had taken.

"Velquez is certainly one of our men," he said, "he'll have you here within twenty minutes."

"How do you know he's your man?" said Temple, "he might be an impostor!"

"Describe him!" snapped Dumas, and there was no mistaking the note of asperity in his voice.

Paul Temple described Velquez.

Dumas said: "You've nothing to worry about, Mr Temple—that's Velquez all right."

Temple put down the receiver, walked out of the telephone booth, and went back to Velquez. Velquez was holding his umbrella over Steve and they appeared to be getting along famously together.

He smiled when he saw Temple approaching.

"Well," said Velquez, "I take it I'm to have the pleasure of your company?"

Temple nodded, grinned, and put his hand in his inside pocket. Both Velquez and Steve expected him to take out his cigarette case: they were not unnaturally surprised when they saw the revolver he was holding. It must be recorded in fact that Velquez was surprised, nervous, agitated, and not a little frightened.

He had good reason to be—the revolver was pointing directly at him.

*

Paul Temple and Steve had left the electric train and were making their way towards the start of the snow run. It was Christmas Eve.

As she started to fasten her skis, Steve said:

"I suppose Velquez—the man who met us at the airport—was a friend of Howell's?"

"A very close friend," said Temple. "The idea, apparently, was to abduct us and hold us as hostages until Howell was released."

"And what about the telephone call? Did you get through to that number Velquez gave you?"

Temple nodded. "I got through all right and the old boy at the other end—a confederate of Velquez's—confirmed that Velquez was a member of the Police."

"Then what made you suspicious?"

Temple smiled. "I described Velquez to his friend as a tall, rather distinguished looking man with spectacles."

"But he didn't wear spectacles!"

"Of course he didn't," said Temple, "but his friend was just a trifle too anxious to be obliging *and immediately jumped to the conclusion that Velquez had disguised himself for the occasion!*"

Steve looked puzzled for a split second, then she began to laugh. She was still laughing when she began her downward swoop with far less caution than her lack of practice warranted. At the first difficult turn she capsized in a smother of white foam, and Temple, barely ten yards behind, was unable to avoid her.

They sat regarding each other for a moment, then Temple managed to regain his feet and went over to give her a hand.

As they brushed the snow off their clothes Paul Temple looked at his wife and grinned.

"We're certainly having a White Christmas!" he said.

SISTER BESSIE OR YOUR OLD LEECH

Cyril Hare

Cyril Hare was a pen-name adopted by Alfred Alexander Gordon Clark (1900–58), who was called to the Bar in 1924. His chambers were in Hare Court, and he lived in Cyril Mansions in Battersea, two addresses that supplied the component parts of his pseudonym. His first crime novel, *Tenant for Death* (1937), was a reworking of a stage play called *Murder in Daylesford Gardens*, and was followed by *Death of a Sportsman* (1938) and the admirably ingenious *Suicide Excepted* (1939). His fourth book, *Tragedy at Law* (1942), is widely regarded as his masterpiece, blending a fascinating and authentic portrayal of life on a legal circuit with an original plot and an unlikely but appealing protagonist in Francis Pettigrew, a barrister whose career, and love life, have proved something of a disappointment. Pettigrew returned in later books, and was rewarded by his creator with a late but happy marriage, and a spell as a judge.

Hare's tragically premature death cut short a crime writing career of distinction; it's a mark of the esteem in which he was held by his fellow practitioners that his friend, the novelist and solicitor Michael Gilbert, edited a collection of his short stories, and that P.D. James referenced one of his cleverest plots in her novel *The Private Patient*. He was an accomplished writer of short stories, many of which were printed in the *Evening Standard*. This story first saw the light of day in that newspaper on 23 December 1949; it has subsequently appeared as 'Your Old Leech' and 'The Present in the Post'.

At Christmas-time we gladly greet
    Each old familiar face.
At Christmas time we hope to meet
    At th' old familiar place.
Five hundred loving greetings, dear,
    From you to me
To welcome in the glad New Year
    I look to see!

H ILDA TRENT TURNED THE CHRISTMAS CARD OVER WITH her carefully manicured fingers as she read the idiotic lines aloud.

"Did you ever hear anything so completely palsied?" she asked her husband. "I wonder who on earth they can get to write the stuff. Timothy, do you know anybody called Leech?"

"Leech?"

"Yes—that's what it says: 'From your old Leech.' Must be a friend of yours. The only Leach I ever knew spelt her name with an a and this one has two e's." She looked at the envelope. "Yes, it was addressed to you. Who is the old Leech?" She flicked the card across the breakfast-table.

Timothy stared hard at the rhyme and the scrawled message beneath it.

"I haven't the least idea," he said slowly.

As he spoke he was taking in, with a sense of cold misery, the fact that the printed message on the card had been neatly altered by hand. The word "Five" was in ink. The original, poet no doubt, had been content with "A hundred loving greetings".

"Put it on the mantelpiece with the others," said his wife. "There's a nice paunchy robin on the outside."

"Damn it, no!" In a sudden access of rage he tore the card in two and flung the pieces into the fire.

It was silly of him, he reflected as he travelled up to the City half an hour later, to break out in that way in front of Hilda; but she would put it down to the nervous strain about which she was always pestering him to take medical advice. Not for all the gold in the Bank of England could he have stood the sight of that damnable jingle on his dining-room mantelpiece. The insolence of it! The cool, calculated devilry! All the way to London the train wheels beat out the maddening rhythm:

"At Christmas-time we gladly greet..."

And he had thought that the last payment had seen the end of it. He had returned from James's funeral triumphant in the certain belief that he had attended the burial of the blood-sucker who called himself "Leech". But he was wrong, it seemed.

"Five hundred loving greetings, dear..."

Five hundred! Last year it had been three, and that had been bad enough. It had meant selling out some holdings at an awkward moment. And now five hundred, with the market in its present state! How in the name of all that was horrible was he going to raise the money?

He would raise it, of course. He would have to. The sickening, familiar routine would be gone through again. The cash in Treasury notes would be packed in an unobtrusive parcel and left in the cloakroom at Waterloo. Next day he would park his car as usual in the railway yard at his local station. Beneath the windscreen wiper—"the old familiar place"—would be tucked the cloakroom ticket. When he came down again from work in the evening the ticket would be gone. And that would be that—till next time. It was the way that Leech preferred it and he had no option but to comply.

The one certain thing that Trent knew about the identity of his blackmailer was that he—or could it be she?—was a member of his family. His family! Thank heaven, they were no true kindred of his. So far as he knew he had no blood relation alive. But "his" family they had been, ever since, when he was a tiny, ailing boy, his father had married the gentle, ineffective Mary Grigson, with her long trail of soft, useless children. And when the influenza epidemic of 1919 carried off John Trent he had been left to be brought up as one of that clinging, grasping clan. He had got on in the world, made money, married money, but he had never got away from the "Grigsons". Save for his stepmother, to whom he grudgingly acknowledged that he owed his start in life, how he loathed them all! But "his" family they remained, expecting to be treated with brotherly affection, demanding his presence at family reunions, especially at Christmas-time.

"At Christmas-time we hope to meet…"

He put down his paper unread and stared forlornly out of the carriage window. It was at Christmas-time, four years before, that the whole thing started—at his stepmother's Christmas Eve party, just such a boring family function as the one he would have to attend in a few days' time. There had been some silly games to amuse the children—Blind Man's Buff and Musical Chairs—and in the course of them his wallet must have slipped from his pocket. He discovered the loss next morning, went round to the house and retrieved it. But when it came into his hands again there was one item missing from its contents. Just one. A letter, quite short and explicit, signed in a name that had about then become fairly notorious in connection with an unsavoury enquiry into certain large-scale dealings in government securities. How he could have been fool enough to keep it a moment longer than was necessary!... but it was no good going back on that.

And then the messages from Leech had begun. Leech had the letter. Leech considered it his duty to send it to the principal of Trent's firm, who was also Trent's father-in-law. But, meanwhile, Leech was a trifle short of money, and for a small consideration... So it had begun, and so, year in and year out, it had gone on.

He had been so sure that it was James! That seedy, unsuccessful stock-jobber, with his gambling debts and his inordinate thirst for whisky, had seemed the very stuff of which blackmailers are made. But he had got rid of James last February, and here was Leech again, hungrier than ever. Trent shifted uneasily in his seat. "Got rid of him" was hardly the right way to put it. One must be fair to oneself. He had merely assisted James to get rid of his worthless self. He had done no more than ask James to dinner at his club, fill him up with whisky and leave him to drive home on a foggy night with the roads treacherous with frost. There had been an unfortunate incident on the Kingston bypass, and that was the end of James—and, incidentally, of two perfect strangers who had happened to be on the road at the same time. Forget it! The point was that the dinner—and the whisky—had been a dead loss. He would not make the same mistake again. This Christmas Eve he intended to make sure who his persecutor was. Once he knew, there would be no half measures.

★

Revelation came to him midway through Mrs John Trent's party—at the very moment, in fact, when the presents were being distributed from the Christmas tree, when the room was bathed in the soft radiance of coloured candles and noisy with the "Oohs!" and "Ahs!" of excited children and with the rustle of hastily unfolded paper parcels. It was so simple, and so unexpected, that he could have laughed aloud. Appropriately enough, it was his own contribution to the party that was responsible. For some time past it had been his unwritten duty, as the prosperous member of the family, to present his stepmother with some delicacy to help out the straitened resources of her house in providing a feast worthy of the occasion. This year, his gift had taken the form of half a dozen bottles of champagne—part of a consignment which he suspected of being corked. That champagne, acting on a head unused to anything stronger than lemonade, was enough to loosen Bessie's tongue for one fatal instant.

Bessie! Of all people, faded, spinsterish Bessie! Bessie, with her woolwork and her charities—Bessie with her large, stupid, appealing eyes and her air of frustration, that put you in mind of a bud frosted just before it could come into flower! And yet, when you came to think of it, it was natural enough. Probably, of all the Grigson tribe, he disliked her the most. He felt for her all the loathing one must naturally feel for a person one has treated badly; and he had been simple enough to believe that she did not resent it.

She was just his own age, and from the moment that he had been introduced into the family had constituted herself his protector against the unkindness of his elder step-brother. She had been, in her revoltingly sentimental phrase, his "own special sister". As they grew up, the roles were reversed, and she became his protégée, the admiring spectator of his early struggles. Then it had become pretty clear that she and everybody else expected him to marry her. He had considered the idea quite seriously for some time. She was pretty enough in those days, and, as the phrase went, worshipped the ground he trod on. But he had had the good sense to see in time that he must look elsewhere if he wanted to make his way in the world. His engagement to Hilda had been a blow to Bessie. Her old-maidish look and her absorption in good works dated from then. But she had been sweetly forgiving—to all appearances. Now, as he stood there under the mistletoe, with a ridiculous paper cap on his head, he marvelled how he could have been so easily deceived. As though, after all, anyone could have written that Christmas card but a woman!

Bessie was smiling at him still—smiling with the confidential air of the mildly tipsy, her upturned shiny nose glowing pink in the candle-light. She had assumed a slightly puzzled expression, as though trying to recollect what she had said. Timothy smiled back and raised his glass to her. He was stone-cold sober, and he could remind her of her words when the occasion arose.

"My present for you, Timothy, is in the post. You'll get it tomorrow, I expect. I thought you'd like a change from those horrid Christmas cards!"

And the words had been accompanied with an unmistakable wink.

"Uncle Timothy!" One of James's bouncing girls jumped up at him and gave him a smacking kiss. He put her down with a grin and tickled her ribs as he did so. He suddenly felt light-hearted and on good terms with all the world—one woman excepted. He moved away from the mistletoe and strolled round the room, exchanging pleasantries with all the family. He could look them in the face now without a qualm. He clicked glasses with Roger, the prematurely aged, overworked G.P. No need to worry now whether his money was going in that direction! He slapped Peter on the back and endured patiently five minutes' confidential chat on the difficulties of the motor-car business in these days. To Marjorie, James's widow, looking wan and ever so brave in her made-over black frock, he spoke just the right words of blended sympathy and cheer. He even found in his pockets some half-crowns for his great, hulking step-nephews. Then he was standing by his stepmother near the fireplace, whence she presided quietly over the noisy, cheerful scene, beaming gentle good nature from her faded blue eyes.

"A delightful evening," he said, and meant it.

"Thanks to you, Timothy, in great part," she replied. "You have always been so good to us."

Wonderful what a little doubtful champagne would do! He would have given a lot to see her face if he were to say: "I suppose you are not aware that your youngest daughter, who is just now pulling a cracker with that ugly little boy of Peter's, is blackmailing me and that I shortly intend to stop her mouth for good?"

He turned away. What a gang they all were! What a shabby, out-at-elbows gang! Not a decently cut suit or a well-turned-out woman among the lot of them! And he had imagined that his money had been going to support some of them! Why, they all simply reeked of honest poverty! He could see it now. Bessie explained everything. It was typical of her twisted mind to wring cash from him by threats and give it all away in charities.

"You have always been so good to us." Come to think of it, his stepmother was worth the whole of the rest put together. She must be hard put to it, keeping up Father's old house, with precious little coming in from her children. Perhaps one day, when his money was really his own again, he might see his way to do something for her... But there was a lot to do before he could indulge in extravagant fancies like that.

Hilda was coming across the room towards him. Her elegance made an agreeable contrast to the get-up of the Grigson women. She looked tired and rather bored, which was not unusual for her at parties at this house.

"Timothy," she murmured, "can't we get out of here? My head feels like a ton of bricks, and if I'm going to be fit for anything tomorrow morning—"

Timothy cut her short.

"You go home straight away, darling," he said. "I can see that it's high time you were in bed. Take the car. I can walk—it's a fine evening. Don't wait up for me."

"You're not coming? I thought you said—"

"No. I shall have to stay and see the party through. There's a little matter of family business I'd better dispose of while I have the chance."

Hilda looked at him in slightly amused surprise.

"Well, if you feel that way," she said. "You seem to be very devoted to your family all of a sudden. You'd better keep an eye on Bessie while you are about it. She's had about as much as she can carry."

Hilda was right. Bessie was decidedly merry. And Timothy continued to keep an eye on her. Thanks to his attentions, by the end of the evening, when Christmas Day had been seen in and the guests were fumbling for their wraps, she had reached a stage when she could barely stand. "Another glass," thought Timothy from the depths of his experience, "and she'll pass right out."

"I'll give you a lift home, Bessie," said Roger, looking at her with a professional eye. "We can just squeeze you in."

"Oh, nonsense, Roger!" Bessie giggled. "I can manage perfectly well. As if I couldn't walk as far as the end of the drive!"

"I'll look after her," said Timothy heartily. "I'm walking myself, and we can guide each other's wandering footsteps home. Where's your coat, Bessie? Are you sure you've got all your precious presents?"

He prolonged his leave-taking until all the rest had gone, then helped Bessie into her worn fur coat and stepped out of the house, supporting her with an affectionate right arm. It was all going to be too deliciously simple.

Bessie lived in the lodge of the old house. She preferred to be independent, and the arrangement suited everyone, especially since James after one of his reverses on the turf had brought his family to live with his mother to save expense. It suited Timothy admirably now. Tenderly he escorted her to the end of the drive, tenderly he assisted her to insert her latchkey in the door, tenderly he supported her into the little sitting-room that gave out of the hall.

There Bessie considerately saved him an enormous amount of trouble and a possibly unpleasant scene. As he put her down upon the sofa she finally succumbed to the champagne. Her eyes closed, her mouth opened and she lay like a log where he had placed her.

Timothy was genuinely relieved. He was prepared to go to any lengths to rid himself from the menace of blackmail, but if he could lay his hands on the damning letter without physical violence he would be well satisfied. It would be open to him to take it out of Bessie in other ways later on. He looked quickly round the room. He knew its contents by heart. It had hardly changed at all since the day when Bessie first furnished her own room when she left school. The same old battered desk stood in the corner, where from the earliest days she had kept her treasures. He flung it open, and a flood of bills, receipts, charitable appeals and yet more charitable appeals came cascading out. One after another, he went through the drawers with ever-increasing urgency, but still failed to find what he sought. Finally he came upon a small inner drawer which resisted his attempts to open it. He tugged at it in vain, and then seized the poker from the fireplace and burst the flimsy lock by main force. Then he dragged the drawer from its place and settled himself to examine its contents.

It was crammed as full as it could hold with papers. At the very top was the programme of a May Week Ball for his last year at Cambridge. Then there were snapshots, press-cuttings—an account of his own wedding among them—and, for the rest, piles of letters, all in his handwriting. The wretched woman seemed to have hoarded every scrap he had ever written to her. As he turned them over, some of the phrases he had used in them floated into his mind, and he began to apprehend for the first time what the depth of her resentment must have been when he threw her over.

But where the devil did she keep the only letter that mattered?

As he straightened himself from the desk he heard close behind him a hideous, choking sound. He spun round quickly. Bessie was standing behind him, her face a mask of horror. Her mouth was wide open in dismay. She drew a long shuddering breath. In another moment she was going to scream at the top of her voice...

Timothy's pent-up fury could be contained no longer. With all his force he drove his fist full into that gaping, foolish face. Bessie went down as though she had been shot and her head struck the leg of a table with the crack of a dry stick broken in two. She did not move again.

Although it was quiet enough in the room after that, he never heard his stepmother come in. Perhaps it was the sound of his own pulses drumming in his ears that had deafened him. He did not even know how long she had been there. Certainly it was long enough for her to take in everything that was to be seen there, for her voice, when she spoke, was perfectly under control.

"You have killed Bessie," she said. It was a calm statement of fact rather than an accusation.

He nodded, speechless.

"But you have not found the letter."

He shook his head.

"Didn't you understand what she told you this evening? The letter is in the post. It was her Christmas present to you. Poor, simple, loving Bessie!"

He stared at her, aghast.

"It was only just now that I found that it was missing from my jewel-case," she went on, still in the same flat, quiet voice. "I don't know how she found out about it, but love—even a crazy love like hers—gives people a strange insight sometimes."

He licked his dry lips.

"Then you were Leech?" he faltered.

"Of course. Who else? How otherwise do you think I could have kept the house open and my children out of debt on my income? No, Timothy, don't come any nearer. You are not going to commit two murders tonight. I don't think you have the nerve in any case, but to be on the safe side I have brought the little pistol your father gave me when he came out of the army in 1918. Sit down."

He found himself crouching on the sofa, looking helplessly up into her pitiless old face. The body that had been Bessie lay between them.

"Bessie's heart was very weak," she said reflectively. "Roger had been worried about it for some time. If I have a word with him,

I daresay he will see his way to issue a death certificate. It will, of course, be a little expensive. Shall we say a thousand pounds this year instead of five hundred? You would prefer that, Timothy, I dare say, to—the alternative?"

Once more Timothy nodded in silence.

"Very well. I shall speak to Roger in the morning—after you have returned me Bessie's Christmas present. I shall require that for future use. You can go now, Timothy."

A BIT OF WIRE-PULLING

E. C. R. Lorac

Edith Caroline Rivett (1894–1958) produced no fewer than seventy-one crime novels, forty-eight of them under the name E.C.R. Lorac, and the remainder as by Carol Carnac. She was born in Hendon, and studied at the Central School of Arts and Crafts. As Lorac, her series detective was Chief Inspector Macdonald, a "London Scot" who made his debut in *The Murder on the Burrows* (1931). Macdonald is a likeable, if lightly sketched, character, and Lorac continued to write about him until the end of her life. Her earlier novels were often set in London; examples include *The Organ Speaks* (1935), which earned a rhapsodic review in the *Sunday Times* from Dorothy L. Sayers, the atmospheric *Bats in the Belfry* (1937), and a lively war-time whodunit, *Murder by Matchlight* (1945). After the Second World War, Lorac moved to the north west of England, and wrote a number of mysteries set around the Lune valley, including *The Theft of the Iron Dogs* (1948); she proved at least as skilled in evoking rural life and landscapes as in describing the scurry and bustle of the capital.

Lorac, who served as Secretary of the Detection Club for a number of years, had a relatively leisurely approach to storytelling which meant that she preferred to make use of the space afforded by a novel to writing short stories. This tale, one of her few attempts at the short mystery, was collected under its present title in *The Evening Standard Detective Book, Series 2* (1951); in its original incarnation in the *Evening Standard* on 11 October 1950, the title was 'Death at the Bridge Table'.

"IT'S A VERY RARE THING FOR A MURDER TO BE COMMITTED actually in the presence of a police officer," said Inspector Lang, the old C.I.D. man.

"I should think it's unique," growled Dr Walton, and Harland (a rising young barrister) put in:

"Tell us the yarn, Inspector. We're a safe audience, and it's just the night for a yarn."

The three men were chance guests at an inn in the Lake District. It was Easter-time, but the weather had turned dirty on them: a shrill north-easter had brought snow and put a stop to rock climbing and walking. That evening, sitting over a grand log fire, the three men had disclosed their callings and were soon deep in mutual "shop".

Inspector Lang stretched out his long legs to the fire. "Aye, it was quite a story," he said, "and it happened on just such a dirty night as this one. You may remember hearing of Sir Charles Leighton—one of the wealthiest industrialists in the north. It all began when Leighton came to the Chief Constable saying he was receiving threatening letters. Not surprising, maybe, because he'd been a harsh old devil in his time. We couldn't trace the writer, and at last Leighton demanded police protection. 'Look here,' he said, 'this last letter tells me I'm for it before the old year's out. Today's December 30th. Now I haven't given the police much trouble during my life. I reckon you can give me police protection until New Year's Day—and if I'm scuppered by some agitator I've sacked it's up to you to catch him.' The Chief Constable said Leighton was a man of some importance and we'd better oblige him. And that's how I went with Sir Charles to a bridge party at his son-in-law's on New Year's Eve. Not that I play bridge—but that didn't matter. I drove with him to Harrowby Manor—poshed up in a dinner jacket and all—and quite an evening I had of it. No one but Sir Charles knew I was a C.I.D. man, of course.

"Sir Charles had but the one surviving child, Annabell," went on the inspector. "She was married to John Bland. He was a financier—clever chap, always able to foretell the markets—so it was said. A lovely house that was, and the young couple—John and Annabell Bland—welcomed us very prettily. Of course, they made a great fuss of Sir Charles, and they accepted me as one of his friends and treated me accordingly. There were six of us altogether—John and Annabell Bland, Sir Charles, a young R.A.F. officer, a pretty lass named Avril Walsh, and yours truly. It was decided that Bland should sit out the first rubber and he made himself very civil to me, while the other four settled down at the bridge table. I sat by the fire, and the bridge table was in the middle of the room. Bland was an attentive son-in-law, and he and his young missis made quite a to-do over seeing Sir Charles was comfortable. He was a big heavy chap, and they gave him a very fine chair—a Jacobean piece it was—strong and heavy enough to take any man's weight. They got settled at last and Sir Charles was in great fettle—he'd bid a slam and was dead keen to make it. John Bland and I chatted quietly so as not to interrupt the game. I said I thought the snow had stopped falling and Bland said: 'I think you're wrong. It's heavier than ever,' and he went to the french window and pulled the curtain back to peer out. The room faced east and the window was pretty well snowed up—just like this one is now—and as Bland peered out he gave a sudden yell: 'Good God! There's a man out there on the verandah! What the hell! Look out, everybody; he's got a gun...' I jumped up, but the shot came hard on Bland's words. The glass tinkled down as the bullet came through and Leighton dropped dead over the table, shot through the head."

"A pretty kettle of fish for you, Inspector," grunted Dr Walton, "with you there on duty to protect Leighton—but did you get the assailant?"

"Aye," said Lang. "I got him—eventually. There was a moment of wild confusion after the shot. Bland tried to get the french window open and to rush outside to grapple with the gunman, but I wouldn't have that—I wasn't risking any amateur interference in this job. I'd got young Sergeant Dixon posted outside and I knew he was a good lad. I tackled Bland and pulled him away from the window, though he was all het up with rage—real mad at me. I told 'em I was a C.I.D. officer and I ordered them all to stay where they were. They were all raging at me: The shot came through the window and Bland had seen the gunman jump for cover in the shrubbery: why the hell had I stopped Bland going after him?"

"Well, I reckon I'd have felt the same in similar circumstances," put in Harland, but the old inspector shook his head.

"I may be a bit old and slow, lad, but I wasn't going to have the pack of them tramping outside there in the snow and mucking everything up. Young Dixon reported in a brace of shakes. He'd been on duty at the angle of the house and his attention had been distracted just before the gunshot, but he'd swung round pretty fast when he heard the report. Bland just swore at Dixon. 'Fast, damn you, you weren't fast enough. I tell you I *saw* the chap jump for the shrubbery. You police blokes make me tired. If the inspector here hadn't interfered I'd have got the devil.' Dixon had found the gun though—an old-type army pistol, not an automatic. It had been dropped in the snow on the path at the edge of the verandah, and there were some big footprints out there in the snow, where someone had stood, and a shuffle of prints leading to the shrubbery. By this time a local constable turned up, and I left him on duty with the party. I wasn't letting one of them move until I'd had time to think."

"I can believe the bridge party didn't think very highly of you at that moment," put in Dr Walton, as the old inspector paused in his narrative.

"Maybe not, maybe not," agreed Lang, "but a little thinking's worth a deal of rushing about, sometimes. And I was puzzled. I went outside to have a look. The footprints in the snow were plain enough—a man *had* stood on the verandah and *had* jumped for the shrubbery, though I could see the thaw had set in and the prints were losing shape. Then I found a rather odd item—a short length of spiral curtain wire, the expanding sort. It was hanging on a branch in the shrubbery, opposite the french window. Might have been irrelevant—or might not. I then studied the window and curtain fitments. When I tackled Bland we'd half torn the blind away and the cord had come adrift, but I saw that the telephone wire entered the house through a hole bored in the window framing." Lang paused and then added: "That was about the lot, but I'll just repeat the essential points. Sir Charles was sitting at the bridge table in the centre of the room when he was shot, in line with the window. The shot came *through* the glass. There were footprints outside the window and on the verandah. The gun had been dropped just clear of the verandah, and I'd found a length of expanding curtain wire, hanging on a branch across the path. An hour or so earlier it had been freezing hard, but now the thaw had set in, and I reckoned I'd got to think this thing out before the thaw altered the conditions. Any of you chaps like to have a smack at sorting it out?"

Harland spoke first. "Obviously Bland, the financier, planned a quick way of getting Leighton's fortune, Bland's wife being Leighton's only child. Bland bribed a gunman to shoot Leighton when the curtain was drawn back. And the gunman got into cover in the shrubbery so fast that Dixon didn't see him jump."

"That won't do," said Dr Walton. "You haven't listened to the evidence. Lang said the window was snowed over—as that window is, over there. In addition, the window would have been misted over inside as the room was very warm. How could the gunman see through that window clearly enough to aim? You go outside here and try it. The thing's impossible."

Old Lang chuckled. "Ay, you're right, Doc. In addition to that, how did Bland *see* the chap on the verandah when the window was snowed up and blurred like that?"

"But you said there were footprints in the driven snow on the verandah," persisted Harland.

"I can explain that one," said Dr Walton. "It *had* been freezing hard. Those footsteps could have been made much earlier in the evening, just as the snow was giving over—evidence all prepared. And a gun could have been dropped there, too. No, maybe that won't do. It was an old-fashioned pistol—could you identify it as the gun that was used to shoot Leighton?" he asked Lang.

"I was pretty sure of it, and later we proved it," said Lang. "It was that gun, none other. Well, Doc, I thought I'd have a quick reconstruction of everything before the thaw altered conditions. I made the party take the positions they were in before the shot was fired, and I had Dixon on the verandah and told him to aim at

Leighton's chair when the police constable drew the curtains apart. It was as I thought. The window was still too opaque with mist and snow for Dixon to aim, and the constable said it was impossible to see anything on the verandah. So there we were, but the shot *had* come through the window and Leighton was killed by it."

"Then it was a booby-trap murder," said Harland. "I remember now. You said Bland had fussed around settling Leighton in a heavy chair. Bland must have got the gun fixed outside on the window frame somehow, trained on to the chair at the right height and angle for Leighton's head, and Bland chose the split second to fire the gun when Leighton was sitting erect. He could have fired the gun by a fine line—salmon line say—running through the hole bored for the telephone wire, and cleared the line away during the schemozzle afterwards. How's that?"

"You haven't explained the essential point," objected Dr Walton. "The gun was found lying in the snow at the edge of the verandah—it was not 'fixed outside', as you put it."

Harland looked rueful: "Yes—rather kippers it," he said, and old Lang laughed.

"You've forgotten my bit of curtain wire, laddy. It's very strong, that wire, and when fully extended it's got a powerful pull—grips like a vice. I worked it out you could lash the gun to the upright of the verandah with the expanding wire and take the last turn of the wire across the mouth of the gun barrel. When the gun was fired—by a line, as the lad suggested—the bullet cut the wire and the gun fell free. And the spiral wire sprang back hard as the tension was suddenly released. Which explained why I found the gun on the path and the wire in the shrubbery."

"Cripes, that was a cunning one!" exclaimed Harland, and Lang went on:

"When I did the reconstruction with the bit of wire, Bland's nerve went. He just gave up arguing. He was properly sold, because he'd thought I was just an old dodderer, some friend of Leighton—never occurred to him I was a C.I.D. man."

Lang paused to relight his pipe. "D'you know what it was made me certain it was phoney?" he asked. "Not the snowy window, not even the wire. It was Dixon. I *knew* Dixon was a good lad and on his toes all the time, and I couldn't believe that when Dixon heard the shot he was so slow in turning round that he neither saw nor heard the man jump from the verandah, across the path and into the shrubbery, when the light from the window was shining out across the path. You see, I believe in the lads I've trained. If Dixon didn't see a man on the verandah, it was because there wasn't a man to see. So I looked for some hankey-pankey, and, by gum, I found it. Just a bit of wire."

Dr Walton chuckled. "Good for you, Inspector. Wire-pulling, eh? They say these financial jugglers are always pulling bits of wire, but their puppets don't always work and the market goes against 'em."

"A bit of wire-pulling," said Harland. "Not a bad title for the yarn, eh?"

PATTERN OF REVENGE

John Bude

John Bude was the pen-name adopted by Ernest Carpenter Elmore (1900–1957), who worked as a school teacher and theatrical producer prior to establishing himself as a full-time author. After writing, under his own name, novels of the fantastic rejoicing in titles such as *The Steel Grubs* (1928), he turned to crime fiction in 1935, with *The Cornish Coast Murder*. He swiftly followed this regional mystery with three others set in equally attractive locations: the Lake District, the Sussex Downs, and Cheltenham. Having found a literary niche, he became an increasingly accomplished practitioner of the traditional detective story; after the Second World War, he located several of his novels in continental Europe, a lively example being *Death on the Riviera* (1952).

Bude played a modest but by no means insignificant part in the history of the genre in Britain, being among the handful of writers who joined with John Creasey to found the Crime Writers' Association at a meeting at the National Liberal Club on Guy Fawkes Night, 1953. The CWA now boasts over eight hundred members based not only in the UK but across the globe, and its Dagger Awards are renowned, but much is owed to the pioneering efforts of men like Creasey and Bude. At the time of his sudden death, he had published thirty crime novels, many of them featuring his series detective, Inspector Meredith. Bude seldom attempted short stories; this rare exception first appeared in *The London Mystery Magazine*, No. 21 in 1954.

T HORD JENSEN WAS THE FINEST MAN ON SKIS IN LEVENDAL. Englishmen of the pre-war era, holidaying in our Norwegian mountains, may remember Thord—for after the tragedy he set up as a ski-ing instructor and did exceeding well for himself. So well, in fact, that when he died in 1945 as the result of an accident, Thord was in a position to leave over three thousand pounds to his hated rival, Olaf Kinck. That, of course, was by way of compensation for what he'd done to Olaf—for when the poor fellow was released from an Oslo jail, three months after Thord's confession, it was not only his heart that was broken but his faith in his fellow-men.

But I anticipate.

Karen Garborg was the cause of the tragedy. She was tall, blonde, blue-eyed, with a cold luminous beauty like that of our Northern Lights. She dazzled most of the young men in Levendal, but favoured only two—Thord Jensen and Olaf Kinck.

For two years she kept them dancing attendance on her—the fair-haired, athletic, good-looking Thord; the saturnine, intelligent, lion-hearted Olaf. I, for one, never questioned which of the two she'd finally accept. For all his fire and wit, as I watched Olaf floundering and dipping through the snow, I knew he hadn't a chance. A girl like Karen Garborg would never marry a man with a wooden leg.

Karen lived alone in an isolated timber cottage on the outskirts of the village. Sometimes it was Thord who came striding through the spruce woods after a visit to the girl... shoulders back, head up, singing like a lark. At others it was Olaf who came jerking out of the forest, his dark eyes glittering with exaltation and a small, secret smile on his lips. If the two men met in the street, they passed without recognition. I sometimes think their hatred of each other was fiercer than their love for Karen Garborg.

There was a heavy fall of snow on the night Karen was murdered...

In the morning Knut Larsen, the postman, found her slumped in the open doorway of the cottage, stabbed through the heart. As the only doctor in Levendal, I was called in by the police to make a medical examination. Rigor mortis and temperature tests showed that the girl had been dead for at least twelve hours. There was only one set of tracks in the fresh-fallen snow that the police couldn't account for—single footprints alternating with deep pock-marks, characteristic of the imprint left by a wooden leg.

The footprint matched up with the sole of the left boot that Olaf Kinck was wearing when the police came to question him. The knife they found—half-buried in the snow beneath the church-yard wall—was unquestionably his. There were fingerprints on its smooth bone handle. Olaf's fingerprints and *only* his.

Six weeks later, still protesting his innocence, Olaf was convicted of the murder, and, as in our country there's no death penalty, he was sentenced to life imprisonment.

He'd served about three years of that sentence when Thord Jensen met with his ski-ing accident. Thord was carried back to the house a dying man. I did what I could to ease his agony and, aware that I could do nothing more, turned to steal from his room. As I gained the door I heard his voice, faint but urgent, calling me back to his bedside. I sat down.

"Doctor," he whispered. "Stay with me a moment. There's something I want to tell you."

"Well. Thord?" I said gently.

"It's to do with Olaf Kinck and… and the woman who'd promised to marry him. I mean, of course, poor Karen Garborg."

"Karen!" I cried. "But you told the police the day after her death that it was *you* she'd accepted, Thord. They were seeking a motive for the crime. Are you claiming that we were wrong… that it *wasn't* jealousy that drove Olaf to murder her?"

"Olaf didn't murder her," said Thord in a low voice. "He's serving a sentence for a crime he didn't commit. *I killed Karen Garborg!*"

"You?"

"Yes, it was I who visited her that night and thrust the knife into her heart."

"But… but it's impossible!" I contested. "All the evidence pointed to the fact that Olaf was the guilty man. It was *his* knife. *His* fingerprints on the handle. *His* footprints in the snow. Above all, there were the tell-tale pock-marks left by his wooden leg. And since Olaf was the only one-legged man in Levendal—"

Thord broke in huskily:

"Olaf Kinck is innocent. You must see to it that they set him free. I haven't long to live… so I beg of you, Doctor, listen carefully to what I have to say…

"For these last three years my conscience has been darkened by the thought of Olaf's suffering. Before I die I must set right the terrible wrong I did him. It was he that Karen really loved. The morning before she died, Olaf went out to her cottage and came away with her promise of marriage. That evening when I dropped in at the inn, everybody knew that Karen, after two years of indecision, had finally chosen Olaf Kinck…

"I was stunned by the news… barely conscious of what I was saying or doing. Olaf was there, celebrating with his friends. He was already drunk, slumped back in his chair, incapable of speech… yet his glances seemed to mock me with silent and triumphant laughter. Then something seemed to crack in my brain…

"One thought was drawn through my head like a thread of fire. If I wasn't to marry Karen, then no man should—least of all Olaf Kinck. I waited, saying nothing, until he left the inn. Then I slipped quietly away and followed him. As I'd anticipated, he didn't get very far down the street before he collapsed in the black shadow of the churchyard wall. I went up to him and shook him. But he just sprawled there, unmoving, in a drunken sleep. The moon was bright on the fresh-fallen snow. It would be easy, I realized, to take the path through the forest to Karen's house. Earlier that evening I'd noticed the hunting-knife at Olaf's belt. I drew it from its sheath with my gloved hand and slipped it into my pocket. Then I knelt down and unlaced his one and only boot.

"It was all so simple and inevitable. I moved faultlessly through the pattern of my revenge. In a little over half an hour Karen Garborg was dead and the boot was back on Olaf's left foot. I thrust the bloodstained knife into the snow a few feet from where he lay unnoticed in the shadows, taking care that the hilt should easily be seen. Then, without meeting a soul, I returned home and waited for the law to take its course.

"The next day, when the police came to question me, I swore that Olaf had lied to his friends at the inn. He'd known that Karen had promised herself to me. He'd known for the simple reason that I'd gone straight to him that afternoon and told him. He'd made for the inn that night, not to celebrate his good-fortune but to drown his grief. They believed me, of course. And why not? Didn't my explanation provide an obvious motive for the murder?" For a moment, exhausted by the effort to lay before me the facts of his astounding story, Thord struggled to get his breath. Then he gasped out: "When Olaf comes out of prison he'll need money. Quick, Doctor... there's pen and paper on my desk. Will you write this for me? Just this... 'I leave all I possess to Olaf Kinck.' Then let me sign it while I still have the strength."

"But, Thord!" I cried, bewildered. "How can this story of yours be true? You've explained about the knife and the fingerprints on the handle. But the single footprints and the pock-marks left by Olaf's wooden leg—what of those?"

"They tell me," said Thord faintly, "that the boot Olaf was wearing on the night of Karen's murder is now in the museum of crime at Oslo."

"Yes," I nodded. "That's true. I've seen it there myself."

"Then you must take another look at it, Doctor, for it's that boot which will unlock the door of Olaf's cell and set him free. You will find three small holes in the sole of that boot... *nail* holes."

"But why? I don't understand."

It occurred to me that his mind was beginning to wander.

"Stilts," he jerked out. "I was always good... on stilts... ever since I was a lad. So very simple, Doctor. All I had to do that night was... was to nail Olaf's boot to my left stilt. The other, you see... in the snow... just like a wooden leg..."

CRIME AT LARK COTTAGE

John Bingham

John Michael Ward Bingham, 7th Earl of Clanmorris (1908–88) was a member of the gentry who, following a spell as a journalist, was recruited into MI5 by Maxwell Knight. One of his younger colleagues was David Cornwell, who was inspired by Bingham's success as an author of fiction to become a novelist himself, under the name John Le Carré. Le Carré has subsequently acknowledged that Bingham was a key inspiration for his most famous character, the spy George Smiley.

Bingham was unquestionably an establishment figure, yet his first crime novel, *My Name is Michael Sibley* (1952), is a bitterly ironic novel about an increasingly menacing police investigation into the death of a man whom Sibley, the narrator, had good cause to hate. He followed this up with *Five Roundabouts to Heaven* (1953; also known as *The Tender Poisoner*), which more than half a century later was made into a good film with a poor title, *Married Life*. *A Fragment of Fear* (1965), a gripping story of suspense and paranoia, was also filmed, in 1970, with David Hemmings and Gayle Hunnicutt in the lead roles. Thereafter, Bingham's career as a crime writer seemed to lose momentum, although his books remained as readable as ever. This rare example of a Bingham short story was first published in the 1954 Christmas Number of *The Illustrated London News*.

T HE WEATHER WAS FOUL. IT HAD BEEN SNOWING, OFF AND on, for some days, but during the last few hours the temperature had suddenly risen, and with the departure of the cold had come the rain, pitting the smooth snow, causing it to fall with soft rustles and sighs from the branches in the coppice which surrounded the cottage on three sides.

Bradley switched off his engine in the black-velvet shadows of the trees opposite the little gate; and went up to the gate, and saw that it bore the name "Lark Cottage"; saw, too, the soft lamplight gleaming through the chinks in the curtains of the front room.

It had been dark for two hours now. A blustery little wind had arisen, sweeping in chilly rushes across the moors, driving the rain before it, and plunging into the little hollow in which the cottage lay.

There was no other habitation in sight.

Bradley unlatched the gate, and walked up a narrow path and knocked on the door. For a few seconds he heard nothing. Then came the sound of footsteps, but they did not come to the door. He heard them pass in front of the door, then begin to ascend uncarpeted stairs.

For a few seconds he stood listening, hearing the water drip from the eaves. A sudden gust of wind and rain, stronger than usual, caused him to turn up the collar of his raincoat.

Suddenly, somewhere above him, a window was opened, and the gust of wind died away, and in the silence that followed a woman's voice said:

"Who is there? What do you want?"

"You don't know me," he replied. "I am sorry to trouble you."

"Who are you?"

"You don't know me," he repeated. "My name is John Bradley. It will mean nothing to you, I'm afraid. I got lost, and now I've developed car trouble. The clutch is slipping badly. I see there is a telephone line to your cottage. I would be most grateful if I could use it. I'll naturally pay you for the call."

He looked up as he spoke. He could see the pale blob of her face in the darkness, peering down at him through the half-opened lattice window. For a second or two she said nothing. Then she said:

"Wait a minute. I'll come down."

He heard her close the window, and the sound of her footsteps on the stairs again, and the noise of the door being unbolted.

He followed her into the little hall, and then into the living-room. The room was a curious mixture of dark oak furniture, solid and enduring, and cheap modern bric-à-brac.

In a far corner a small Christmas tree, obviously dug from the garden, stood in a red pot. A little girl, aged about ten, was decorating it with bits of silver tinsel. As he came in she held in her hand a small Fairy Queen, made of cardboard, and painted with some silvery, glittering substance.

She was fair-haired and pale, and looked at him gravely, uncer-tainly; poised, as though prepared to drop everything and run at the first harsh word.

Unhappy, thought Bradley; thin and unhappy, and none too fit. Aloud, he said:

"That's a pretty tree you have."

For a second, warmth crept into the child's face and lit up the grey eyes, and she seemed about to speak. Then, as the woman spoke, the child thought better of it, and the face assumed again its former cautious expression.

"The 'phone's on the window-sill."

Bradley swung round and looked at the woman. She was about thirty-five, tall and sallow, with dark hair and eyes, the hair brushed back severely from the forehead. Her features were regular and, but for the fact that she was thin, and that her face wore a harsh, embittered expression, he would have considered her handsome for her age. Bradley said:

"I suppose Skandale is the nearest town? Can you recommend a garage there?"

She shook her head. "You won't get a garage to come out at this time of night." She paused and added: "I doubt if there's even a garage open, now, in that dump."

"You are not from these parts?"

She shook her head again and said:

"I come from Brighton."

Bradley said: "You must find it a bit different up here." But she was not listening to him. She was standing rigid, her head slightly on one side, as though she were listening. Her neck, her arms, her legs, her whole body was stiff. Bradley, glancing at her hands, saw that they were clenched and pressed to her sides.

But the child was different.

The child's face was suddenly flushed and eager. She had stopped trying to fix the Fairy Queen to the top of the Christmas tree, and had turned her head towards the window, towards the front of the house and the garden path, and the gate through which a man would normally approach the cottage. She said:

"Did you hear anything, Mummy?"

The question seemed to break the tension. The woman said sharply:

"Julia! Either get on with your tree or go to bed—one or the other."

The child turned back to her tree, but almost at once turned her head quickly to the window.

Bradley heard the click of the gate, too. So did the woman. The noise came during a momentary lull in the wind, so when the woman said it was the storm blowing the gate nobody believed her, and the child ran to the window and looked out, thrusting the curtains aside, and peering into the night, kneeling on the window-seat, nose pressed against the pane. Bradley said:

"You are expecting somebody, perhaps? Well, I won't bother you any longer. I'll be on my way. Maybe the clutch will last a mile or two, and I'll do the last stretch on foot. I take it this road leads to the main road to Skandale?"

The woman was staring towards the window, towards the child. Bradley thought: The child is eager, expectant, but the mother is afraid. At last she said:

"It is at least ten miles to Skandale. You would do better to stay here, Mr Bradley, and catch the early-morning bus from the end of the lane. I can give you a bed."

"But if you are expecting somebody—"

"Nobody is coming."

There was a flurry of movement on the window-seat, as the child Julia swung round and cried:

"But, Mummy, it said on the wireless—"

"Julia! Come, it's time for your bed."

She went to the window and took the child by the hand, and

jerked the child off the window-seat and towards the door. At the
door she paused a moment and said:

"You are quite welcome to stay the night. Julia and I share the
same room, and I will make up the bed in the small room for you."

Bradley caught the strained, almost eager undertone in her
voice, and knew that she wanted him to stay; knew that she was
afraid, and wished for his company in the house; afraid, even
though as yet she had not said what she feared—or whom.

"Very well," he said mildly. "I will gladly stay. It is very kind
of you."

He watched her lead the child out of the room, and heard them
mount the stairs, and the sound of voices in an upper room, the
woman's sharp and scolding, the child's plaintive. Then he went
quickly to the window and looked out.

The light from the room was reflected by the snow, so that he
could dimly see the garden and the path and the gate. But there
was no sign of anybody.

He had not expected to see anybody.

He lit a cigarette and wandered slowly round the room, glancing at the books in the bookshelf near the fireplace, at the cheap
water-colours on the whitewashed walls.

On a table near the window stood a small silver tray. He picked
it up and read the inscription in the middle, written in the impec-
cable copybook handwriting peculiar to such things:

TO FRED SHAW ON HIS MARRIAGE—
FROM HIS PALS AT THE MILL.

He replaced the tray and moved to the fireplace, noting the inex-
pensive china ornaments, the walnut-wood clock. In a light oak

frame was a picture of a plump-faced man with fair, receding hair. In the bottom right-hand corner were the words: "To Lucy, with love from Leslie."

He wandered on, looking for something which he somehow knew he would not find; looking for the usual wedding picture, the wedding picture of Fred and Lucy Shaw.

He was not in the least surprised not to find it; not in the least surprised to find no trace of Fred Shaw at all, except for the silver tray, and that, after all, was worth money.

No trace, that is, until he came to the newspaper lying on the dark oak sideboard, and saw the double-column headlines, and read the text about Frederick Shaw, and how warders and police were scouring the countryside for him.

Frederick Shaw, aged forty-two. Escaped from Larnforth Prison.

Shaw, the murderer, reprieved because of what Home Secretaries call "just an element of doubt"; and serving a life sentence, with nine-tenths of it still to run.

Shaw, the former overseer, respected in all Skandale, who once or twice a year got a little befuddled with beer; who was known to be on bad terms with his uncle, the Skandale jeweller.

Good-natured old Fred Shaw, who never could explain how his cap and heavy blackthorn stick were found beside the battered body of the jeweller—or even what became of the money they alleged he had stolen.

Bradley put the paper down quickly when he heard the footsteps on the stairs. Too quickly. As he turned away, the big pages slipped over the side of the polished sideboard. So that when Lucy Shaw came into the room, she saw it lying on the floor, and said:

"So now you know, I suppose?"

"Yes," said Bradley, "I know all right."

Now that the need for acting was past, she stood in front of the fireplace, massaging one hand with the other, staring at him with frightened eyes. A tall, gaunt woman, with a wide, sensual mouth. The harsh expression had left her face. He saw her lips quiver.

"What are you scared of, Mrs Shaw?" asked Bradley.

"I'm not scared, I'm not at all scared. What should I be frightened of?"

"That's what I was asking," said Bradley. He moved to the door and said: "I'll go and get my suitcase out of the car."

He went into the hall and out of the front door and down the garden path to the car. She heard the sound of the car door being slammed. On the way back, he paused by the front door. Then he came into the hall and put down his suitcase.

When he came into the living-room he said:

"Come outside a minute, will you?"

She swung round and stared at him.

"Why?"

"Did your husband—did Mr Shaw use a walking-stick much?"

"He always used one—almost always. He was a bit lame from a mill accident. Why?" And when he did not answer, when he only looked at her without saying anything, she repeated loudly, almost shrilly: "Why?"

"Well, come outside a minute," repeated Bradley, and groped in his trenchcoat pocket for his torch. She walked into the hall, and when she hesitated by the front door he said: "Come on, it's all right. I'm with you, and I'm six foot tall and quite strong."

The wind had dropped now, but the rain still fell; but softly, soundlessly, more in the nature of a moorland mist.

The snow was becoming soft on the surface, but was still deep, so that the footprints round the house showed up very distinctly in the light of the torch; so did the small ferrule-holes in the snow on the left-hand side of the prints.

"I suppose he was left-handed," said Bradley, more to himself than to Lucy Shaw, and saw her nod almost imperceptibly. He raised the torch-beam a trifle and said: "See how he turned aside to look into the room? I suppose he saw me in there with you and Julia. I suppose he is waiting for me to go. Then he will come in and spend a few short hours with you, and perhaps take some clothes and money and go."

He heard a movement by his side, and looked round, and found she had gone back into the house.

When he joined her in the living-room she was sitting crouched in a chair by the fire. Her sallow face had turned white. She was trembling violently.

Bradley said: "I think l had better go, after all. I'm keeping him out in the night rain. It's the police job to catch escaped convicts, not mine. I was a prisoner of war once. I've got a sneaking sympathy for them. Poor devil!" he added softly.

But she jumped to her feet, and clutched him by both arms, and said shrilly: "You mustn't go! Please don't go!" A thought struck her, and she added, almost in a whisper: "Before the gate clicked—you remember?—the child and I heard a sound. I think it was his hand, perhaps his finger-nail on the window-pane, as he looked in through a chink in the curtains."

Bradley said: "I'm going, unless you tell me why you are afraid."

He pushed her from him, and she went and stood by the fireplace. After a while she said:

"He thought I should have done more for him when he had his trial. He said he was with me at the time of the murder, and I should have said so too.

"But he wasn't, so I couldn't say it, could I? After all, you're on oath, aren't you, Mr Bradley?"

"You're on oath all right."

"So I couldn't go and perjure myself, could I? I mean, could I?"

"Men don't kill women for *not* doing something, Mrs Shaw." He glanced at the grate. "The fire is dying, and there is no more wood. Where is it kept?"

She looked up at him, fear in her eyes, and said:

"In the shed near the back door. I can't go out there and fetch it. I'm not going out there alone."

"I'll fetch it. Just come with me and show me where it is. Just come to the kitchen door with me."

He opened the kitchen door, and she stood with him, and pointed to the shed, a few yards away. The rain still fell, still soundlessly. Somewhere some water was running gurgling down a drain. Otherwise there was no noise, either in the trees which pressed down upon the cottage or in the glistening bushes which edged their way to within a few feet of the back door.

He shone his torch, first on the shed then on the bushes, and took a step forward, and suddenly stopped as the bushes shook violently and snow cascaded from them.

Behind him he heard Lucy Shaw gasp and sob twice.

"It's probably only a rabbit," said Bradley, and walked towards the bushes. For a second he shone his torch at them, then made his way to the shed and gathered a trugful of sawn logs, and came back towards the kitchen.

Lucy Shaw stood watching him, afraid to go back into the house alone, afraid to go out into the night with him. She kept passing her hand over her smooth hair, nervously, restlessly, staring out into the night at him with her black, dilated eyes.

The crash of the broken window, the broken living-room window, made her turn and scream; caused Bradley to break into a run; and woke up the child. Bradley heard her calling: "Mummy! Mummy! What's that?"

Bradley carried the trug with one hand and with the other pushed Lucy Shaw into the house and whispered fiercely:

"Tell her I dropped a vase! Go on, tell her that!"

When the woman had done so, they went into the living-room and saw the stone with the piece of paper wrapped round it, lying among the shattered fragments of window-pane. Bradley picked it up and smoothed out the paper, and saw, in capital letters, the word, ADULTERESS. He handed it to Lucy Shaw and said:

"He doesn't seem to think an awful lot of you, does he?"

The curtains were stirring in front of the jagged hole in the window. Bradley flung the logs down by the side of the fire and said abruptly:

"I've had enough of this! I'm going. You can sort it out yourself with your husband. It's no affair of mine."

She flung herself at the door, ashen-faced, and stood in front of it, barring his way.

"You can't leave me here—alone!"

"Who can't?" asked Bradley tonelessly, and watched the curtains billowing into the room as a sudden gust of wind struck them.

"Where are the police?" gasped Lucy Shaw. "Surely the first thing they do is to send men to watch an escaped convict's home?"

Bradley pointed to the telephone.

"Ring 'em up and tell 'em so. Ask them where they are," he said. "Go on—ring them up."

She ran to the telephone and lifted the receiver, and listened. When a few seconds had gone by, Bradley said:

"Perhaps the wire is down with the snow. Perhaps he's cut it—you never know. They do it in books."

After a minute, the operator answered. Lucy Shaw held her breath for a few seconds to control her voice, to try to restrain the tremor. Then she said:

"I want the police! Tell the police to come! This is Mrs Shaw, Lark Cottage, Oak Lane, off the Skandale-Tollbrook road. Tell them it's—it's very urgent! My life is in danger! My—there's an escaped convict—a murderer—trying to get in!"

She replaced the receiver and stared at Bradley. He glanced at his watch and said:

"They'll probably be here in half an hour. Three-quarters, at the most. You'll be all right till then, I expect."

He moved towards the door.

She did not move, unable to believe that he was really going.

"It's no business of mine," he pointed out for the second time. And when she clung to him and began to whimper, he said:

"Don't be daft. He won't *kill* you for not perjuring yourself at his trial. He won't even kill you for carrying on with this podgy-faced, blond brute." He waved towards the picture on the chimney-piece.

"Maybe he'll black your eye. Maybe he won't even do that, once he's in the house and you can appeal to him. Men are queer that way."

But she clung to the door-handle, gaunt and unlovely, her black hair now in disarray, and when he tried to move her hands she suddenly flung herself against him, temporarily forcing him away from the door, and said:

"It's worse than that. He knew Leslie and I were in love, long before his uncle was killed."

"So what?" said Bradley, and moved again towards the door.

"You fool!" gasped Lucy Shaw. "Don't you understand what I'm trying to tell you? Leslie—Leslie Bond—traveller for Fred's firm, killed the old man, and stole the money, and planted the evidence against my husband, Fred Shaw—and I knew he had done it!"

"Did you now?" said Bradley mildly. "What's that to me?"

"And I let Fred go on trial for it, and I'd have let him die for it, too—and he knows it, and that's why he'll kill me if you go before the police arrive!"

"Fancy!" said Bradley, staring at her. "And your friend, where is he?"

"He left the country, saying he would come back when the case had blown over."

"And will he?"

"No!" said Lucy Shaw bitterly.

"Not voluntarily!"

As she spoke, her voice rose almost to a scream, and Bradley, watching the hatred flush her sallow face and stretch her mouth into a thin, straight line, knew that the end was at hand.

"Where is he?" he asked abruptly.

"In Melbourne, Australia, and I'll damn well tell the police when they arrive!"

"You may be charged as an accomplice after the fact."

"What the hell do I care!" shouted Lucy Shaw. "I'm not going to be done-in to-night, nor twenty years hence, to save Leslie Bond, and I don't care who knows it!"

Bradley said, woodenly: "If that's the way you feel, and since you wish to make a statement, I don't mind telling you now that the police are here already."

Lucy Shaw looked round. "Where?"

"Here," said Bradley, and put his hand in his raincoat pocket and produced his warrant-card. Almost automatically his voice reverted to a routine drone as he continued: "I am Superintendent Bradley, of Scotland Yard. Sergeant Wood, I believe, has been listening outside that broken window. If you wish to make a written statement, I have some foolscap sheets of paper and a pen.

"I must, however, warn you that you are not obliged to do so, and that anything you say, or any written statement you make from now onwards, may be used in evidence against you. I should perhaps add that your husband was recaptured some three hours ago within a few miles of the prison."

"What with you skylarking around, trespassing, making footprints, and breaking windows," said Superintendent Bradley later to Sergeant Wood, "and me extorting confessions through fear and subterfuge, there's been enough crime committed at Lark Cottage to-night to fill a sheaf of charge-sheets.

"Funny, how I always had an uneasy feeling about that case, even though I did collect the evidence which put Frederick Shaw in the dock. Lucky she didn't attend the trial and know my face."

He filled his pipe and added: "The kid'll be glad to be back with her father for Christmas. I reckon she hated her mother. So did I, if it comes to that," he said, striking a match.

"And so did I," said Sergeant Wood. "I was frozen stiff."

'TWIXT THE CUP AND THE LIP

Julian Symons

Julian Gustave Symons (1912–1994) was a major figure in the British crime fiction world in the second half of the twentieth century. In addition to being a respected poet, historian, and biographer, he was an incisive critic of the genre, and his account of the evolution of crime fiction, *Bloody Murder*, which ran to four editions, was characteristically lucid and enjoyable. Symons was Chair of the Crime Writers' Association, and later President of the Detection Club; in addition, he received the genre's two principal lifetime achievement awards, winning the CWA Diamond Dagger and becoming a Mystery Writers of America Grand Master.

As a novelist, Symons received the CWA Gold Dagger for *The Colour of Murder* (1957), yet for all his many garlands, his fiction is nowadays apt to be regrettably under-valued. This may in part be because he had an antipathy towards series detectives, although a few characters, such as the barrister Magnus Newton and the actor Sheridan Haynes, appear in more than one of his books. His criticism of some classic detective fiction (he dismissed the likes of John Rhode as "Humdrums") masks the reality that his own mystery fiction was often markedly ingenious; examples include *The Players and the Game* (1972) and *The Plot against Roger Rider* (1973). His early short stories, which featured an inquiry agent called Francis Quarles, often boast neat twists, although in later years, his short fiction focused increasingly on psychological suspense. This story was included in *Ellery Queen's Mystery Magazine* in January 1965.

"A BEAUTIFUL MORNING, MISS OLIPHANT. I SHALL TAKE A short constitutional."

"Very well, Mr Payne."

Mr Rossiter Payne put on his good thick Melton overcoat, took his bowler hat off its peg, carefully brushed it, and put it on. He looked at himself in a small glass and nodded approvingly at what he saw.

He was a man in his early fifties, but he might have passed for ten years less, so square were his shoulders, so ruler-straight his back. Two fine wings of grey hair showed under the bowler. He looked like a retired Guards officer, although he had, in fact, no closer relationship with the Army than an uncle who had been cashiered.

At the door he paused, his eyes twinkling. "Don't let anybody steal the stock while I'm out, Miss Oliphant."

Miss Oliphant, a thin spinster of indeterminate middle-age, blushed. She adored Mr Payne.

He had removed his hat to speak to her. Now he clapped it on his head again, cast an appreciative look at the bow window of his shop, which displayed several sets of standard authors with the discreet legend above—*Rossiter Payne, Bookseller. Specialist in First Editions and Manuscripts*—and made his way up New Bond Street toward Oxford Street.

At the top of New Bond Street he stopped, as he did five days a week, at the stall on the corner. The old woman put the carnation into his buttonhole.

"Fourteen shopping days to Christmas now, Mrs Shankly. We've all got to think about it, haven't we?"

A ten shilling note changed hands instead of the usual half crown. He left her blessing him confusedly.

This was perfect December weather—crisply cold, the sun shining. Oxford Street was wearing its holiday decorations—enormous gold and silver coins from which depended ropes of pearls, diamonds, rubies, emeralds. When lighted up in the afternoon they looked pretty, although a little garish for Mr Payne's refined taste. But still, they had a certain symbolic feeling about them, and he smiled at them.

Nothing, indeed, could disturb Mr Payne's good temper this morning—not the jostling crowds on the pavements or the customary traffic jams which seemed, indeed, to please him. He walked along until he came to a large store that said above it, in enormous letters, ORBIN'S. These letters were picked out in coloured lights, and the lights themselves were festooned with Christmas trees and holly wreaths and the figures of the Seven Dwarfs, all of which lighted up.

Orbin's department store went right round the corner into the comparatively quiet Jessiter Street. Once again Mr Payne went through a customary ceremony. He crossed the road and went down several steps into an establishment unique of its kind—Danny's Shoe Parlour. Here, sitting on a kind of throne in this semi-basement, one saw through a small window the lower halves of passers-by. Here Danny, with two assistants almost as old as himself, had been shining shoes for almost 30 years.

Leather-faced, immensely lined, but still remarkably sharp-eyed, Danny knelt down now in front of Mr Payne, turned up the cuffs of his trousers, and began to put an altogether superior shine on already well-polished shoes.

"Lovely morning, Mr Payne."

"You can't see much of it from here."

"More than you think. You see the pavements, and if they're not spotted, right off you know it isn't raining. Then there's something in the way people walk, you know what I mean, like it's Christmas in the air." Mr Payne laughed indulgently. Now Danny was mildly reproachful. "You still haven't brought me in that pair of black shoes, sir."

Mr Payne frowned slightly. A week ago he had been almost knocked down by a bicyclist, and the mudguard of the bicycle had scraped badly one of the shoes he was wearing, cutting the leather at one point. Danny was confident that he could repair the cut so that it wouldn't show. Mr Payne was not so sure.

"I'll bring them along," he said vaguely.

"Sooner the better, Mr Payne, sooner the better."

Mr Payne did not like being reminded of the bicycle incident. He gave Danny half a crown instead of the ten shillings he had intended, crossed the road again, and walked into the side entrance of Orbin's, which called itself unequivocally "London's Greatest Department Store."

This end of the store was quiet. He walked up the stairs, past the grocery department on the ground floor, and wine and cigars on the second, to jewellery on the third. There were rarely many people in this department, but today a small crowd had gathered around a man who was making a speech. A placard at the department entrance said: "The Russian Royal Family Jewels. On display for two weeks by kind permission of the Grand Duke and Grand Duchess of Moldo-Lithuania."

These were not the Russian Crown Jewels, seized by the Bolsheviks during the Revolution, but an inferior collection brought out of Russia by the Grand Duke and Grand Duchess, who had long since become plain Mr and Mrs Skandorski, who lived in New Jersey, and were now on a visit to England.

Mr Payne was not interested in Mr and Mrs Skandorski, nor in Sir Henry Orbin who was stumbling through a short speech. He was interested only in the jewels. When the speech was over he mingled with the crowd round the showcase that stood almost in the middle of the room.

The royal jewels lay on beds of velvet—a tiara that looked too heavy to be worn, diamond necklaces and bracelets, a cluster of diamonds and emeralds, and a dozen other pieces, each with an elegant calligraphic description of its origin and history. Mr Payne did not see the jewels as a romantic relic of the past, nor did he permit himself to think of them as things of beauty. He saw them as his personal Christmas present.

He walked out of the department, looking neither to left nor right, and certainly paying no attention to the spotty young clerk who rushed forward to open the door for him. He walked back to his bookshop, sniffing that sharp December air, made another little joke to Miss Oliphant, and told her she could go out to lunch. During her lunch hour he sold an American a set of a Victorian magazine called *The Jewel Box*.

It seemed a good augury.

In the past ten years Mr Payne had engineered successfully— with the help of other, and inferior, intellects—six jewel robberies. He had remained undetected, he believed, partly because of his skill in planning, partly because he ran a perfectly legitimate book business, and partly because he broke the law only when he needed money. He had little interest in women, and his habits were generally ascetic, but he did have one vice.

Mr Payne developed a system at roulette, an improvement on the almost infallible Frank-Konig system, and every year he went to Monte Carlo and played his system. Almost every year it failed—or rather, it revealed certain imperfections which he then tried to remedy.

It was to support his foolproof system that Mr Payne had turned from bookselling to crime. He believed himself to be, in a quiet way, a mastermind in the modern criminal world.

Those associated with him were far from that, as he immediately would have acknowledged. He met them two evenings after he had looked at the royal jewels, in his pleasant little flat above the shop, which could be approached from a side entrance opening into an alley.

There was Stacey, who looked what he was, a thick-nosed thug; there was a thin young man in a tight suit whose name was Jack Line, and who was always called Straight or Straight Line; and there was Lester Jones, the spotty clerk in the Jewellery Department.

Stacey and Straight Line sat drinking whisky, Mr Payne sipped some excellent sherry, and Lester Jones drank nothing at all, while Mr Payne in his pedantic, almost schoolmasterly manner, told them how the robbery was to be accomplished.

"You all know what the job is, but let me tell you how much it is worth. In its present form the collection is worth whatever sum you'd care to mention—a quarter of a million pounds perhaps. There is no real market value. But alas, it will have to be broken up. My friend thinks the value will be in the neighbourhood of fifty thousand pounds. Not less, and not much more."

"Your friend?" the jewellery clerk said timidly.

"The fence. Lambie, isn't it?" It was Stacey who spoke. Mr Payne nodded. "Okay, how do we split?"

"I will come to that later. Now, here are the difficulties. First of all, there are two store detectives on each floor. We must see to it that those on the third floor are not in the Jewellery Department. Next, there is a man named Davidson, an American, whose job it is to keep an eye on the jewels. He has been brought over here by a protection agency, and it is likely that he will carry a gun. Third, the jewels are in a showcase, and any attempt to open this showcase other than with the proper key will set off an alarm. The key is kept in the Manager's Office, inside the Jewellery Department."

Stacey got up, shambled over to the whiskey decanter, and poured himself another drink. "Where do you get all this from?"

Mr Payne permitted himself a small smile. "Lester works in the department. Lester is a friend of mine."

Stacey looked at Lester with contempt. He did not like amateurs.

"Let me continue, and tell you how the obstacles can be overcome. First, the two store detectives. Supposing that a small fire bomb were planted in the Fur Department, at the other end of the third floor from Jewellery—that would certainly occupy one detective for a few minutes. Supposing that in the department that deals with ladies' hats, which is next to Furs, a woman shopper complained that she had been robbed—this would certainly involve the other store detective. Could you arrange this, Stace? These—assistants, shall I call them?—would be paid a straight fee. They would have to carry out their diversions at a precise time, which I have fixed as ten thirty in the morning."

"Okay," said Stacey. "Consider it arranged."

"Next, Davidson. He is an American, as I said, and Lester tells me that a happy event is expected in his family any day now. He has left Mrs Davidson behind in America, of course. Now, supposing that a call came through, apparently from an American hospital, for Mr Davidson. Supposing that the telephone in the Jewellery Department was out of order because the cord had been cut. Davidson would be called out of the department for the few minutes, no more, that we should need."

"Who cuts the cord?" Stacey asked.

"That will be part of Lester's job."

"And who makes the phone call?"

"Again, Stace, I hoped that you might be able to provide—"

"I can do that." Stacey drained his whiskey. "But what do you do?"

Mr Payne's lips, never full, were compressed to a disapproving line. He answered the implied criticism only by inviting them to look at two maps—one the layout of the entire third floor, the other of the Jewellery Department itself. Stacey and Straight were impressed, as the uneducated always are, by such evidence of careful planning.

"The Jewellery Department is at one end of the third floor. It has only one exit—into the Carpet Department. There is a service lift which comes straight up into the Jewellery Department. You and I, Stace, will be in that. We shall stop it between floors with the Emergency Stop button. At exactly ten thirty-two we shall go up to the third floor. Lester will give us a sign. If everything has gone well, we proceed. If not, we call the job off. Now, what I propose…"

He told them, they listened, and they found it good. Even the ignorant, Mr Payne was glad to see, could recognize genius. He told Straight Line his role.

"We must have a car, Straight, and a driver. What he has to do is simple, but he must stay cool. So I thought of you." Straight grinned.

"In Jessiter Street, just outside the side entrance to Orbin's, there is a parking space reserved for Orbins' customers. It is hardly ever full. But if it is full you can double park there for five minutes—cars often do that. I take it you can—acquire a car, shall I say?—for the purpose. You will face away from Oxford Street, and you will have no more than a few minutes' run to Lambie's house on Greenly Street. You will drop Stace and me, drive on a mile or two, and leave the car. We shall give the stuff to Lambie. He will pay on the nail. Then we all split."

From that point they went on to argue about the split. The argument was warm, but not really heated. They settled that Stacey would get 25 per cent of the total, Straight and Lester 12 ½ per cent each, and that half would go to the mastermind. Mr Payne agreed to provide out of his share the £150 that Stacey said would cover the three diversions.

The job was fixed six days ahead—for Tuesday of the following week.

Stacey had two faults which had prevented him from rising high in his profession. One was that he drank too much, the other that he was stupid. He made an effort to keep his drinking under control, knowing that when he drank he talked. So he did not even tell his wife about the job, although she was safe enough.

But he could not resist cheating about the money, which Payne had given to him in full.

The fire bomb was easy. Stacey got hold of a little man named Shrimp Bateson, and fixed it with him. There was no risk, and Shrimp thought himself well paid with twenty-five quid. The bomb itself cost only a fiver, from a friend who dealt in hardware. It was guaranteed to cause just a little fire, nothing serious.

For the telephone call Stacey used a Canadian who was grubbing a living at a striptease club. It didn't seem to either of them that the job was worth more than a tenner, but the Canadian asked for twenty and got fifteen.

The woman was a different matter, for she had to be a bit of an actress, and she might be in for trouble since she actually had to cause a disturbance. Stacey hired an eighteen-stone Irish woman named Lucy O'Malley, who had once been a female wrestler, and had very little in the way of a record—nothing more than a couple of drunk and disorderlies. She refused to take anything less than £50, realizing, as the others hadn't, that Stacey must have something big on.

The whole lot came to less than £100, so that there was cash to spare. Stacey paid them all half their money in advance, put the rest of the £100 aside, and went on a roaring drunk for a couple of days, during which he somehow managed to keep his mouth buttoned and his nose clean.

When he reported on Monday night to Mr Payne he seemed to have everything fixed, including himself.

Straight Line was a reliable character, a young man who kept himself to himself. He pinched the car on Monday afternoon, took it along to the semilegitimate garage run by his father-in-law, and put new license plates on it. There was no time for a respray job, but he roughed the car up a little so that the owner would be unlikely to recognize it if by an unlucky chance he should be passing outside Orbin's on Tuesday morning. During this whole operation, of course, Straight wore gloves.

He also reported to Mr Payne on Monday night.

*

Lester's name was not really Lester—it was Leonard. His mother
and his friends in Balham, where he had been born and brought
up, called him Lenny. He detested this, as he detested his surname
and the pimples that, in spite of his assiduous efforts with oint-
ment, appeared on his face every couple of months. There was
nothing he could do about the name of Jones, because it was on
his National Insurance card, but Lester for Leonard was a gesture
toward emancipation.

Another gesture was made when he left home and mother for
a one room flat in Notting Hill Gate. A third gesture—and the
most important one—was his friendship with Lucille, whom he
had met in a jazz club called The Whizz Fizz.

Lucille called herself an actress, but the only evidence of it was
that she occasionally sang in the club. Her voice was tuneless but
loud. After she sang, Lester always bought her a drink, and the
drink was always whiskey.

"So what's new?" she said. "Lester-boy, what's new?"

"I sold a diamond necklace today. Two hundred and fifty
pounds. Mr Marston was very pleased." Mr Marston was the
manager of the Jewellery Department.

"So Mr Marston was pleased. Big deal." Lucille looked round
restlessly, tapping her foot.

"He might give me a raise."

"Another ten bob a week and a pension for your fallen arches."

"Lucille, won't you—"

"No." The peak of emancipation for Lester, a dream beyond
which his thoughts really could not reach, was that one day Lucille
would come to live with him. Far from that, she had not even slept
with him yet. "Look, Lester-boy, I know what I want, and let's face
it, you haven't got it."

He was incautious enough to ask, "What?"

"Money, moolah, the green folding stuff. Without it you're nothing, with it they can't hurt you."

Lester was drinking whiskey too, although he didn't really like it. Perhaps, but for the whiskey, he would never have said, "Supposing I had money?"

"What money? Where would you get it—draw it out of the Savings Bank?"

"I mean a lot of money."

"Lester-boy, I don't think in penny numbers. I'm talking about real money."

The room was thick with smoke; the Whizz Fizz Kids were playing. Lester leaned back and said deliberately, "Next week I'll have money—thousands of pounds."

Lucille was about to laugh. Then she said, "It's my turn to buy a drink, I'm feeling generous. Hey, Joe. Two more of the same."

Later that night they lay on the bed in his one-room flat. She had let him make love to her, and he had told her everything.

"So the stuff's going to a man called Lambie in Greenly Street?"

Lester had never before drunk so much in one evening. Was it six whiskies or seven? He felt ill, and alarmed. "Lucille, you won't say anything? I mean, I wasn't supposed to tell—"

"Relax. What do you take me for?" She touched his cheek with red-tipped nails. "Besides, we shouldn't have secrets, should we?"

He watched her as she got off the bed and began to dress. "Won't you stay? I mean, it would be all right with the landlady."

"No can do, Lester-boy. See you at the club, though. Tomorrow night. Promise."

"Promise." When she had gone he turned over on to his side and groaned. He feared that he was going to be sick, and he was. Afterwards, he felt better.

Lucille went home to her flat in Earl's Court which she shared with a man named Jim Baxter. He had been sent to Borstal for a robbery from a confectioner's which had involved considerable violence. Since then he had done two short stretches. He listened to what she had to say, then asked, "What's this Lester like?"

"A creep."

"Has he got the nerve to kid you, or do you think it's on the level, what he's told you?"

"He wouldn't kid me. He wants me to live with him when he's got the money. I said I might."

Jim showed her what he thought of that idea. Then he said, "Tuesday morning, eh. Until then, you play along with this creep. Any change in plans I want to know about it. You can do it, can't you, baby?"

She looked up at him. He had a scar on the left side of his face which she thought made him look immensely attractive. "I can do it. And Jim?"

"Yes?"

"What about afterwards?"

"Afterwards, baby? Well, for spending money there's no place like London. Unless it's Paris."

Lester Jones also reported on Monday night. Lucille was being very kind to him, so he no longer felt uneasy.

Mr Payne gave them all a final briefing and stressed that timing, in this as in every similar affair, was the vital element.

★

Mr Rossiter Payne rose on Tuesday morning at his usual time, just after eight o'clock. He bathed and shaved with care and precision, and ate his usual breakfast of one soft-boiled egg, two pieces of toast, and one cup of unsugared coffee. When Miss Oliphant arrived he was already in the shop.

"My dear Miss Oliphant. Are you, as they say, ready to cope this morning?"

"Of course, Mr Payne. Do you have to go out?"

"I do. Something quite unexpected. An American collector named—but I mustn't tell his name even to you, he doesn't want it known—is in London, and he has asked me to see him. He wants to try to buy the manuscripts of—but there again I'm sworn to secrecy, although if I weren't I should surprise you. I am calling on him, so I shall leave things in your care until—" Mr Payne looked at his expensive watch—"not later than midday. I shall certainly be back by then. In the meantime, Miss Oliphant, I entrust my ware to you."

She giggled. "I won't let anyone steal the stock, Mr Payne."

Mr Payne went upstairs again to his flat where, laid out on his bed, was a very different set of clothes from that which he normally wore. He emerged later from the little side entrance looking quite unlike the dapper, retired Guards officer known to Miss Oliphant.

His clothes were of the shabby nondescript ready-to-wear kind that might be worn by a City clerk very much down on his luck—the sleeve and trouser cuffs distinctly frayed, the tie a piece of dirty string. Curling strands of rather disgustingly gingery hair strayed from beneath his stained grey trilby hat and his face was grey too—grey and much lined, the face of a man of sixty who has been defeated by life.

Mr Payne had bright blue eyes, but the man who came out of the side entrance had, thanks to contact lenses, brown ones. This man shuffled off down the alley with shoulders bent, carrying a rather dingy suitcase. He was quite unrecognizable as the upright Rossiter Payne.

Indeed, if there was a criticism to be made of him, it was that he looked almost too much the "little man." Long, long ago, Mr Payne had been an actor, and although his dramatic abilities were extremely limited, he had always loved and been extremely good at make-up.

He took with him a realistic-looking gun that, in fact, fired nothing more lethal than caps. He was a man who disliked violence, and thought it unnecessary.

After he left Mr Payne on Monday night, Stacey had been unable to resist having a few drinks. The alarm clock wakened him to a smell of frizzling bacon. His wife sensed that he had a job on, and she came into the bedroom as he was taking the Smith and Wesson out of the cupboard.

"Bill." He turned round. "Do you need that?"

"What do you think?"

"Don't take it."

"Ah, don't be stupid."

"Bill, please. I get frightened."

Stacey put the gun into his hip pocket. "Won't use it. Just makes me feel a bit more comfortable, see?"

He ate his breakfast with a good appetite and then telephoned Shrimp Bateson, Lucy O'Malley, and the Canadian, to make sure they were ready. They were. His wife watched him fearfully. Then he came to say goodbye.

"Bill, look after yourself."

"Always do." And he was gone.

*

Lucille had spent Monday night with Lester. This was much against her wish, but Jim had insisted on it, saying that he must know of any possible last-minute change.

Lester had no appetite at all. She watched with barely concealed contempt as he drank no more than half a cup of coffee and pushed aside his toast. When he got dressed his fingers were trembling so that he could hardly button his shirt.

"Today's the day, then."

"Yes. I wish it was over."

"Don't worry."

He said eagerly, "I'll see you in the club tonight."

"Yes."

"I shall have the money then, and we could go away together. Oh, no, of course not—I've got to stay on the job."

"That's right," she said, humouring him.

As soon as he had gone, she rang Jim and reported that there were no last-minute changes.

Straight Line lived with his family. They knew he had a job on, but nobody talked about it. Only his mother stopped him at the door and said, "Good luck, son," and his father said, "Keep your nose clean."

Straight went to the garage and got out the Jag.

10:30.

Shrimp Bateson walked into the Fur Department with a brown-paper package under his arm. He strolled about pretending to look at furs, while trying to find a place to put down the little parcel. There were several shoppers and he went unnoticed.

He stopped at the point where Furs led to the stairs, moved into a window embrasure, took the little metal cylinder out of its brown-paper wrapping, pressed the switch which started the mechanism, and walked rapidly away.

He had almost reached the door when he was tapped on the shoulder. He turned. A clerk was standing with the brown paper in his hand.

"Excuse me, sir, I think you've dropped something. I found this paper—"

"No, no," Shrimp said. "It's not mine."

There was no time to waste in arguing. Shrimp turned and half walked, half ran, through the doors and to the staircase. The clerk followed him. People were coming up the stairs, and Shrimp, in a desperate attempt to avoid them, slipped and fell, bruising his shoulder.

The clerk was standing hesitantly at the top of the stairs when he heard the *whoosh* of sound and, turning, saw flames. He ran down the stairs then, took Shrimp firmly by the arm and said, "I think you'd better come back with me, sir."

The bomb had gone off on schedule, setting fire to the window curtains and to one end of a store counter. A few women were screaming, and other clerks were busy saving the furs. Flack, one of the store detectives, arrived on the spot quickly, and organized the use of the fire extinguishers. They got the fire completely under control in three minutes.

The clerk, full of zeal, brought Shrimp along to Flack. "Here's the man who did it."

Flack looked at him. "Firebug, eh?"

"Let me go. I had nothing to do with it."

"Let's talk to the manager, shall we?" Flack said, and led Shrimp away.

The time was now 10:39.

*

Lucy O'Malley looked at herself in the glass, and at the skimpy hat perched on her enormous head. Her fake-crocodile handbag, of a size to match her person, had been put down on a chair nearby.

"What do you feel, madam?" the young saleswoman asked, ready to take her cue from the customer's reaction.

"Terrible."

"Perhaps it isn't really you."

"It looks bloody awful," Lucy said. She enjoyed swearing, and saw no reason why she should restrain herself.

The salesgirl laughed perfunctorily and dutifully, and moved over again toward the hats. She indicated a black hat with a wide brim. "Perhaps something more like this?"

Lucy looked at her watch. 10:31. It was time. She went across to her handbag, opened it, and screamed.

"Is something the matter, madam?"

"I've been robbed!"

"Oh, really, I don't think that can have happened."

Lucy had a sergeant-major's voice, and she used it. "Don't tell me what can and can't have happened, young woman. My money was in here, and now it's gone. Somebody's taken it."

The salesgirl, easily intimidated, blushed. The department supervisor, elegant, eagle-nosed, blue-rinsed, moved across like an arrow and asked politely if she could help.

"My money's been stolen," Lucy shouted. "I put my bag down for a minute, twenty pounds in it, and now it's gone. That's the class of people they get in Orbin's." She addressed this last sentence to another shopper, who moved away hurriedly.

"Let's look, shall we, just to make sure." Blue Rinse took hold of the handbag, Lucy took hold of it too, and somehow the bag's contents spilled onto the carpet.

"You stupid fool," Lucy roared.

"I'm sorry, madam," Blue Rinse said icily. She picked up handkerchief, lipstick, powder compact, tissues. Certainly there was no money in the bag. "You're sure the money was in the bag?"

"Of course I'm sure. It was in my purse. I had it five minutes ago. Someone here has stolen it."

"Not so loud, please, madam."

"I shall speak as loudly as I like. Where's your store detective, or haven't you got one?"

Sidley, the other detective on the third floor, was pushing through the little crowd that had collected. "What seems to be the matter?"

"This lady says twenty pounds has been stolen from her handbag." Blue Rinse just managed to refrain from emphasizing the word "lady."

"I'm very sorry. Shall we talk about it in the office?"

"I don't budge until I get my money back." Lucy was carrying an umbrella, and she waved it threateningly. However, she allowed herself to be led along to the office. There the handbag was examined again and the salesgirl, now tearful, was interrogated. There also Lucy, having surreptitiously glanced at the time, put a hand into the capacious pocket of her coat, and discovered the purse. There was twenty pounds in it, just as she had said.

She apologized, although the apology went much against the grain for her, declined the suggestion that she should return to the hat counter, and left the store with the consciousness of a job well done.

"Well," Sidley said. "I shouldn't like to tangle with her on a dark night."

The time was now 10:40.

The clock in the Jewellery Department stood at exactly 10:33 when a girl came running in, out of breath, and said to the manager. "Oh, Mr Marston, there's a telephone call for Mr Davidson. It's from America."

Marston was large, and inclined to be pompous. "Put it through here, then."

"I can't. There's something wrong with the line in this department—it seems to be dead."

Davidson had heard his name mentioned, and came over to them quickly. He was a crew-cut American, tough and lean. "It'll be about my wife, she's expecting a baby. Where's the call?"

"We've got it in Administration, one floor up."

"Come on, then." Davidson started off at what was almost a run, and the girl trotted after him. Marston stared at both of them disapprovingly. He became aware that one of his clerks, Lester Jones, was looking rather odd.

"Is anything the matter, Jones? Do you feel unwell?"

Lester said that he was all right. The act of cutting the telephone cord had filled him with terror, but with the departure of Davidson he really did feel better. He thought of the money—and of Lucille.

Lucille was just saying goodbye to Jim Baxter and his friend Eddie Grain. They were equipped with an arsenal of weapons, including flick knives, bicycle chains, and brass knuckles. They did not, however, carry revolvers.

"You'll be careful," Lucille said to Jim.

"Don't worry. This is going to be like taking candy from a baby, isn't it, Eddie?"

"S'right," Eddie said. He had a limited vocabulary, and an almost perpetual smile. He was a terror with a knife.

The Canadian made the call from the striptease club. He had a girl with him. He had told her that it would be a big giggle. When he heard Davidson's voice—the time was just after ten thirty-four—he said, "Is that Mr Davidson?"

"Yes."

"This is the James Long Foster Hospital in Chicago, Mr Davidson, Maternity floor."

"Yes?"

"Will you speak up, please. I can't hear you very well."

"Have you got some news of my wife?" Davidson said loudly. He was in a small booth next to the store switchboard. There was no reply. "Hello? Are you there?"

The Canadian put one hand over the receiver, and ran the other up the girl's bare thigh. "Let him stew a little." The girl laughed. They could hear Davidson asking if they were still on the line. Then the Canadian spoke again.

"Hello, hello, Mr Davidson. We seem to have a bad connection."

"I can hear you clearly. What news is there?"

"No need to worry, Mr Davidson. Your wife is fine."

"Has she had the baby?"

The Canadian chuckled. "Now, don't be impatient. That's not the kind of thing you can hurry, you know."

"What have you got to tell me then? Why are you calling?"

The Canadian put his hand over the receiver again, said to the girl, "You say something."

"What shall I say?"

"Doesn't matter—that we've got the wires crossed or something."

The girl leaned over, picked up the telephone. "This is the operator. Who are you calling?"

In the telephone booth sweat was running off Davidson. He hammered with his fist on the wall of the booth. "Damn you, get off the line! Put me back to the Maternity floor."

"This is the operator. Who do you want, please?"

Davidson checked himself suddenly. The girl had a Cockney voice. "Who are you? What's your game?"

The girl handed the telephone back to the Canadian, looking frightened. "He's on to me."

"Hell." The Canadian picked up the receiver again, but the girl had left it, uncovered, and Davidson had heard the girl's words. He dropped the telephone, pushed open the door of the booth, and raced for the stairs. As he ran he loosened the revolver in his hip pocket.

The time was now 10:41.

Straight Line brought the Jaguar smoothly to a stop in the space reserved for Orbin's customers, and looked at his watch. It was 10:32.

Nobody questioned him, nobody so much as gave him a glance. Beautiful, he thought, a nice smooth job, really couldn't be simpler. Then his hands tightened on the steering wheel.

He saw in the rear-view mirror, standing just a few yards behind him, a policeman. Three men were evidently asking the policeman for directions, and the copper was consulting a London place map.

Well, Straight thought, he can't see anything of me except my back, and in a couple of minutes he'll be gone. There was still plenty of time. Payne and Stacey weren't due out of the building until 10:39 or 10:40. Yes, plenty of time.

But there was a hollow feeling in Straight's stomach as he watched the policeman in his mirror.

Some minutes earlier, at 10:24, Payne and Stacey had met at the service elevator beside the Grocery Department on the ground floor. They had met this early because of the possibility that the elevator might be in use when they needed it, although from Lester's observation it was used mostly in the early morning and late afternoon.

They did not need the elevator until 10:30, and they would be very unlucky if it was permanently in use at that time. If they were that unlucky—well, Mr Payne had said with the pseudo-philosophy of the born gambler, they would have to call the job off. But even as he said this he knew that it was not true, and that having gone so far he would not turn back.

The two men did not speak to each other, but advanced steadily toward the elevator by way of inspecting chow mein, hymettus honey, and real turtle soup. The Grocery Department was full of shoppers, and the two men were quite unnoticed. Mr Payne reached the elevator first and pressed the button. They were in luck. The door opened.

Within seconds they were both inside. Still neither man spoke. Mr Payne pressed the button which said 3, and then, when they had passed the second floor, the button that said Emergency Stop. Jarringly the elevator came to a stop. It was now immobilized, so far as a call from outside was concerned. It could be put back into motion only by calling in engineers who would free the Emergency Stop mechanism—or, of course, by operating the elevator from inside.

Stacey shivered a little. The elevator was designed for freight, and therefore roomy enough to hold twenty passengers; but Stacey had a slight tendency to claustrophobia which was increased by the thought that they were poised between floors. He said, "I suppose that bloody thing will work when you press the button?"

"Don't worry, my friend. Have faith in me." Mr Payne opened the dingy suitcase, revealing as he did so that he was now wearing rubber gloves. In the suitcase were two long red cloaks, two fuzzy white wigs, two thick white beards, two pairs of outsize horn-rimmed spectacles, two red noses, and two hats with large tassels. "This may not be a perfect fit for you, but I don't think you can deny that it's a perfect disguise."

They put on the clothes, Mr Payne with the pleasure he always felt in dressing up, Stacey with a certain reluctance. The idea was clever, all right, he had to admit that, and when he looked in the elevator's small mirror and saw a Santa Claus looking back at him, he was pleased to find himself totally unrecognizable. Deliberately he took the Smith and Wesson out of his jacket and put it into the pocket of the red cloak.

"You understand, Stace, there is no question of using that weapon."

"Unless I have to."

"There is no question," Mr Payne repeated firmly. "Violence is never necessary. It is a confession that one lacks intelligence."

"We got to point it at them, haven't we? Show we mean business."

Mr Payne acknowledged that painful necessity by a downward twitch of his mouth, undiscernible beneath the false beard.

"Isn't it time, yet?"

Mr Payne looked at his watch. "It is now ten twenty-nine. We go—over the top, you might call it—at ten thirty-two precisely. Compose yourself to wait, Stace."

Stacey grunted. He could not help admiring his companion, who stood peering into the small glass, adjusting his beard and moustache, and settling his cloak more comfortably. When at last Mr Payne nodded, and said, "Here we go," and pressed the button marked 3, resentment was added to admiration. He's all right now, but wait till we get to the action, Stacey thought. His gloved hand on the Smith and Wesson reassured him of strength and efficiency.

The elevator shuddered, moved upward, stopped. The door opened. Mr Payne placed his suitcase in the open elevator door so that it would stay open and keep the elevator at the third floor. Then they stepped out.

To Lester the time that passed after Davidson's departure and before the elevator door opened was complete and absolute torture.

The whole thing had seemed so easy when Mr Payne had outlined it to them. "It is simply a matter of perfect timing," he had said. "If everybody plays his part properly, Stace and I will be back in the lift within five minutes. Planning is the essence of this, as of every scientific operation. Nobody will be hurt, and nobody will suffer financially except—" and here he had looked at Lester with a twinkle in his frosty eyes—"except the insurance company. And I don't think the most tender-hearted of us will worry too much about the insurance company."

That was all very well, and Lester had done what he was supposed to do, but he hadn't really been able to believe that the rest of it would happen. He had been terrified, but with the terror was mixed a sense of unreality.

He still couldn't believe, even when Davidson went to the telephone upstairs, that the plan would go through without a hitch. He was showing some costume jewellery to a thin old woman who kept roping necklaces around her scrawny neck, and while he did so he kept looking at the elevator, above which was the department clock. The hands moved slowly, after Davidson left, from 10:31 to 10:32.

They're not coming, Lester thought. It's all off. A flood of relief, touched with regret but with relief predominating, went through him. Then the elevator door opened, and the two Santa Clauses stepped out. Lester started convulsively.

"Young man," the thin woman said severely, "it doesn't seem to me that I have your undivided attention. Haven't you anything in blue and amber?"

It had been arranged that Lester would nod to signify that Davidson had left the department, or shake his head if anything had gone wrong. He nodded now as though he had St Vitus's Dance.

The thin woman looked at him, astonished. "Young man, is anything the matter?"

"Blue and amber," Lester said wildly, "amber and blue." He pulled out a box from under the counter and began to look through it. His hands were shaking.

Mr Payne had been right in his assumption that no surprise would be occasioned by the appearance of two Santa Clauses in any department at this time of year. This, he liked to think, was his own characteristic touch—the touch of, not to be unduly modest about it, creative genius. There were a dozen people in the Jewellery Department, half of them looking at the Russian

Royal Family Jewels, which had proved less of an attraction than Sir Henry Orbin had hoped. Three of the others were wandering about in the idle way of people who are not really intending to buy anything, and the other three were at the counters, where they were being attended to by Lester, a salesgirl whose name was Miss Glenny, and by Marston himself.

The appearance of the Santa Clauses aroused only the feeling of pleasure experienced by most people at sight of these slightly artificial figures of jollity. Even Marston barely glanced at them. There were half a dozen Santa Clauses in the store during the weeks before Christmas, and he assumed that these two were on their way to the Toy Department, which was also on the third floor, or to Robin Hood in Sherwood Forest tableau, which was this year's display for children.

The Santa Clauses walked across the floor together as though they were in fact going into Carpets and then on to the Toy Department, but after passing Lester they diverged. Mr Payne went to the archway that led from Jewellery to Carpets, and Stacey abruptly turned behind Lester toward the Manager's Office.

Marston, trying to sell an emerald brooch to an American who was not at all sure his wife would like it, looked up in surprise. He had a natural reluctance to make a fuss in public, and also to leave his customer; but when he saw Stacey with a hand actually on the door of his own small but sacred office he said to the American, "Excuse me a moment, sir," and said to Miss Glenny, "Look after this gentleman, please"—by which he meant that the American should not be allowed to walk out with the emerald brooch—and called out, although not so loudly that the call could be thought of as anything so vulgar as a shout, "Just a moment, please. What are you doing there? What do you want?"

Stacey ignored him. In doing so he was carrying out Mr Payne's specific instructions. At some point it was inevitable that the people in the department would realize that a theft was taking place, but the longer they could be kept from realizing it, Mr Payne had said, the better. Stacey's own inclination would have been to pull out his revolver at once and terrorize anybody likely to make trouble; but he did as he was told.

The Manager's Office was not much more than a cubbyhole, with papers neatly arranged on a desk; behind the desk, half a dozen keys were hanging on the wall. The showcase key, Lester had said, was the second from the left, but for the sake of appearances Stacey took all the keys. He had just turned to go when Marston opened the door and saw the keys in Stacey's hand.

The manager was not lacking in courage. He understood at once what was happening and, without speaking, tried to grapple with the intruder. Stacey drew the Smith and Wesson from his pocket and struck Marston hard with it on the forehead. The manager dropped to the ground. A trickle of blood came from his head.

The office door was open, and there was no point in making any further attempt at deception. Stacey swung the revolver around and rasped, "Just keep quiet, and nobody else will get hurt."

Mr Payne produced his cap pistol and said, in a voice as unlike his usual cultured tones as possible, "Stay where you are. Don't move. We shall be gone in five minutes."

Somebody said, "Well, I'm damned." But no one moved. Marston lay on the floor, groaning. Stacey went to the showcase, pretended to fumble with another key, then inserted the right one. The case opened at once. The jewels lay naked and unprotected. He dropped the other keys on the floor, stretched in his gloved hands, picked up the royal jewels, and stuffed them into his pocket.

It's going to work, Lester thought unbelievingly, it's going to work. He watched, fascinated, as the cascade of shining stuff vanished into Stacey's pocket. Then he became aware that the thin woman was pressing something into his hand. Looking down, he saw with horror that it was a large, brand-new clasp knife, with the dangerous-looking blade open.

"Bought it for my nephew," the thin woman whispered. "As he passes you, go for him."

It had been arranged that if Lester's behaviour should arouse the least suspicion he should make a pretended attack on Stacey, who would give him a punch just severe enough to knock him down. Everything had gone so well, however, that this had not been necessary, but now it seemed to Lester that he had no choice.

As the two Santa Clauses backed across the room toward the service elevator, covering the people at the counters with their revolvers, one real and the other a toy, Lester launched himself feebly at Stacey, with the clasp knife demonstratively raised. At the same time Marston, on the other side of Stacey and a little behind him, rose to his feet and staggered in the direction of the elevator.

Stacey's contempt for Lester increased with the sight of the knife, which he regarded as an unnecessary bit of bravado. He shifted the revolver to his left hand, and with his right punched Lester hard in the stomach. The blow doubled Lester up. He dropped the knife and collapsed to the floor, writhing in quite genuine pain.

The delivery of the blow delayed Stacey so that Marston was almost up to him. Mr Payne, retreating rapidly to the elevator, shouted a warning, but the manager was on Stacey, clawing at his robes. He did not succeed in pulling off the red cloak, but his other hand came away with the wig, revealing Stacey's own cropped brown hair. Stacey snatched back the wig, broke away, and fired the revolver with his left hand.

Perhaps he could hardly have said himself whether he intended to hit Marston, or simply to stop him. The bullet missed the manager and hit Lester, who was rising on one knee. Lester dropped again. Miss Glenny screamed, another woman cried out, and Marston halted.

Mr Payne and Stacey were almost at the elevator when Davidson came charging in through the Carpet Department entrance. The American drew the revolver from his pocket and shot, all in one swift movement. Stacey fired back wildly. Then the two Santa Clauses were in the service elevator, and the door closed on them.

Davidson took one look at the empty showcase, and shouted to Marston, "Is there an emergency alarm that rings downstairs?"

The manager shook his head. "And my telephone's not working."

"They've cut the line." Davidson raced back through the Carpet Department to the passenger elevators.

Marston went over to where Lester was lying, with half a dozen people round him, including the thin woman. "We must get a doctor."

The American he had been serving said, "I am a doctor." He was bending over Lester, whose eyes were wide open.

"How is he?"

The American lowered his voice. "He got it in the abdomen."

Lester seemed to be trying to raise himself up. The thin woman helped him. He sat up, looked around, and said, "Lucille." Then blood suddenly rushed out of his mouth, and he sank back.

The doctor bent over again, then looked up. "I'm very sorry. He's dead."

The thin woman gave Lester a more generous obituary than he deserved. "He wasn't a very good clerk, but he was a brave young man."

Straight Line, outside in the stolen Jag, waited for the policeman to move. But not a bit of it. The three men with the policeman were pointing to a particular spot on the map, and the copper was laughing; they were having some sort of stupid joke together. What the hell. Straight thought, hasn't the bleeder got any work to do, doesn't he know he's not supposed to be hanging about?

Straight looked at his watch. 10:34, coming up to 10:35—and now, as the three men finally moved away, what should happen but that a teen-age girl should come up, and the copper was bending over toward her with a look of holiday good-will.

It's no good, Straight thought, I shall land them right in his lap if I stay here. He pulled away from the parking space, looked again at his watch. He was obsessed by the need to get out of the policeman's sight.

Once round the block, he thought, just once round can't take more than a minute, and I've got more than two minutes to spare. Then if the copper's still here I'll stay a few yards away from him with my engine running.

He moved down Jessiter Street and a moment after Straight had gone, the policeman, who had never even glanced at him, moved away too.

By Mr Payne's plan they should have taken off their Santa Claus costumes in the service elevator and walked out at the bottom as the same respectable, anonymous citizens who had gone in; but as soon as they were inside the elevator Stacey said, "He hit me." A stain showed on the scarlet right arm of his robe.

Mr Payne pressed the button to take them down. He was proud that, in this emergency, his thoughts came with clarity and logic. He spoke them aloud.

"No time to take these off. Anyway, they're just as good a disguise in the street. Straight will be waiting. We step out and into the car, take them off there. Davidson shouldn't have been back in that department for another two minutes."

"I gotta get to a doctor."

"We'll go to Lambie's first. He'll fix it." The elevator whirred downward. Almost timidly, Mr Payne broached the subject that worried him most. "What happened to Lester?"

"He caught one." Stacey was pale.

The elevator stopped. Mr Payne adjusted the wig on Stacey's head. "They can't possibly be waiting for us, there hasn't been time. We just walk out. Not too fast, remember. Casually, normally."

The elevator door opened and they walked the fifty feet to the Jessiter Street exit. They were delayed only by a small boy who rushed up to Mr Payne, clung to his legs and shouted that he wanted his Christmas present. Mr Payne gently disengaged him, whispered to his mother, "Our tea break. Back later," and moved on.

Now they were outside in the street. But there was no sign of Straight or the Jaguar.

Stacey began to curse. They crossed the road from Orbin's, stood outside Danny's Shoe Parlour for a period that seemed to both of them endless, but was, in fact, only thirty seconds. People looked at them curiously—two Santa Clauses wearing false noses—but they did not arouse great attention. They were oddities, yes, but oddities were in keeping with the time of year and Oxford Street's festive decorations.

"We've got to get away," Stacey said. "We're sitting ducks."

"Don't be a fool. We wouldn't get a hundred yards."

"Planning," Stacey said bitterly. "Fine bloody planning. If you ask me—"

"Here he is."

The Jag drew up beside them, and in a moment they were in and down Jessiter Street, away from Orbin's. Davidson was on the spot less than a minute later, but by the time he had found passers-by who had seen the two Santa Clauses get into the car, they were half a mile away.

Straight Line began to explain what had happened, Stacey swore at him, and Mr Payne cut them both short.

"No time for that. Get these clothes off, talk later."

"You got the rocks?"

"Yes, but Stace has been hit. By the American detective. I don't think it's bad, though."

"Whatsisname, Lester, he okay?"

"There was trouble. Stace caught him with a bullet."

Straight said nothing more. He was not one to complain about something that couldn't be helped. His feelings showed only in the controlled savagery with which he manoeuvred the Jag.

While Straight drove, Mr Payne was taking off his own Santa Claus outfit and helping Stacey off with his. He stuffed them, with the wigs and beards and noses, back into the suitcase. Stacey winced as the robe came over his right arm, and Mr Payne gave him a handkerchief to hold over it. At the same time he suggested that Stacey hand over the jewels, since Mr Payne would be doing the negotiating with the fence. It was a mark of the trust that both men still reposed in Mr Payne that Stacey handed them over without a word, and that Straight did not object or even comment.

They turned into the quiet Georgian terrace where Lambie lived. "Number Fifteen, right-hand side," Mr Payne said.

Jim Baxter and Eddie Grain had been hanging about in the street for several minutes. Lucille had learned from Lester what car Straight was driving. They recognized the Jag immediately, and strolled toward it. They had just reached the car when it came to a stop in front of Lambie's house. Stacey and Mr Payne got out.

Jim and Eddie were not, after all, too experienced. They made an elementary mistake in not waiting until Straight had driven away. Jim had his flick knife out and was pointing it at Mr Payne's stomach.

"Come on now, Dad, give us the stuff and you won't get hurt," he said.

On the other side of the car Eddie Grain, less subtle, swung at Stacey with a shortened length of bicycle chain. Stacey, hit round the head, went down, and Eddie was on top of him, kicking, punching, searching.

Mr Payne hated violence, but he was capable of defending himself. He stepped aside, kicked upward, and knocked the knife flying from Jim's hand. Then he rang the doorbell of Lambie's house. At the same time Straight got out of the car and felled Eddie Grain with a vicious rabbit punch.

During the next few minutes several things happened simultaneously. At the end of the road a police whistle was blown, loudly and insistently, by an old lady who had seen what was going on.

Lambie, who also saw what was going on and wanted no part of it, told his manservant on no account to answer the doorbell or open the door.

Stacey, kicked and beaten by Eddie Grain, drew his revolver and fired four shots. One of them struck Eddie in the chest, and another hit Jim Baxter in the leg. Eddie scuttled down the street holding his chest, turned the corner, and ran slap into the arms of two policemen hurrying to the scene.

Straight, who did not care for shooting, got back into the Jag and drove away. He abandoned the Jag as soon as he could, and went home.

When the police arrived, with a bleating Eddie in tow, they found Stacey and Jim Baxter on the ground, and several neighbours only too ready to tell confusing stories about the great gang fight that had just taken place. They interrogated Lambie, of course, but he had not seen or heard anything at all.

And Mr Payne? With a general melee taking place, and Lambie clearly not intending to answer his doorbell, he had walked away down the road. When he turned the corner he found a cab, which he took to within a couple of hundred yards of his shop. Then, an anonymous man carrying a shabby suitcase, he went in through the little side entrance.

Things had gone badly, he reflected as he again became Mr Rossiter Payne the antiquarian bookseller, mistakes had been made. But happily they were not his mistakes. The jewels would be hot, no doubt; they would have to be kept for a while, but all was not lost.

Stace and Straight were professionals—they would never talk. And although Mr Payne did not, of course, know that Lester was dead, he realized that the young man would be able to pose as a wounded hero and was not likely to be subjected to severe questioning.

So Mr Payne was whistling *There's a Silver Lining* as he went down to greet Miss Oliphant.

"Oh, Mr Payne," she trilled. "You're back before you said. It's not half-past eleven."

Could that be true? Yes, it was.

"Did the American collector—I mean, will you be able to sell him the manuscripts?"

"I hope so. Negotiations are proceeding, Miss Oliphant. They may take some time, but I hope they will reach a successful conclusion."

The time passed uneventfully until 2:30, in the afternoon when Miss Oliphant entered his little private office. "Mr Payne, there are two gentlemen to see you. They won't say what it's about, but they look—well, rather funny."

As soon as Mr Payne saw them and even before they produced their warrant cards, he knew that there was nothing funny about them. He took them up to the flat and tried to talk his way out of it, but he knew it was no use. They hadn't yet got search warrants, the Inspector said, but they would be taking Mr Payne along anyway. It would save them some trouble if he would care to show them—

Mr Payne showed them. He gave them the jewels and the Santa Claus disguises. Then he sighed at the weakness of subordinates. "Somebody squealed, I suppose."

"Oh, no. I'm afraid the truth is you were a bit careless."

"*I* was careless." Mr Payne was genuinely scandalized.

"Yes. You were recognized."

"Impossible!"

"Not at all. When you left Orbin's and got out into the street, there was a bit of a mixup so that you had to wait. Isn't that right?"

"Yes, but I was completely disguised."

"Danny the shoeshine man knows you by name, doesn't he?"

"Yes, but he couldn't possibly have seen me."

"He didn't need to. Danny can't see any faces from his basement, as you know, but he did see something, and he came to tell us about it. He saw two pairs of legs, and the bottoms of some sort of red robes. And he saw the shoes. He recognized one pair of shoes, Mr Payne. Not those you're wearing now, but that pair on the floor over there."

Mr Payne looked across the room at the black shoes—shoes so perfectly appropriate to the role of shabby little clerk that he had been playing, and at the decisive, fatally recognizable sharp cut made by the bicycle mudguard in the black leather.

BRITISH LIBRARY CRIME CLASSICS

Many of our titles are also available in eBook and audio editions